The passing motorcyclist gave her a cheeky grin and winked.

Caitlin shook her head at his audacity—then saw a car swerve. Heard a sickening *thud* as it hit the biker.

When the man at her feet moaned, still alive, she breathed, "Thank You, Lord."

He stared up at her. "Hey, angel, you found me," he murmured, grabbing her hand. Then his face twisted in pain. When his eyes fluttered open again, he gasped, "You're praying for me?"

"Yes, I am," Caitlin replied.

"You're wasting your time," he said, teeth clenched against the pain.

"No, I'm not," she whispered, reassured by the touch of God's hand on the situation—the welcome wail of an ambulance siren.

The stranger squeezed her hand. "Who are you, angel?"

"I'm Caitlin. Tell me your name. Stay with me."

But though his hand clung tightly, he didn't answer.

"Please, Lord, ke
aloud. "Keep him

CAROLYNE AARSEN

and her husband, Richard, live on a small ranch in northern Alberta, where they have raised four children and numerous foster children, and are still raising cattle. Carolyne crafts her stories in an office with a large west-facing window through which she can watch the changing seasons while struggling to make her words obey.

A Family-Style Christmas

Carolyne Aarsen

Love Inspired

Recycling programs for this product may not exist in your area.

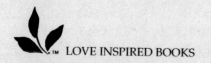 LOVE INSPIRED BOOKS

ISBN-13: 978-0-373-78687-9

A FAMILY-STYLE CHRISTMAS

www.LoveInspiredBooks.com

Printed in U.S.A.

As a mother comforts her child,
so I will comfort you.
—*Isaiah* 66:13

This book is dedicated to all foster parents,
official and unofficial. May God give you the
strength and love you need.

I owe a big thank-you to Anne Canadeo,
who has been an encouraging and inspiring editor
on my first four books. I also want to thank
my new editor, Ann Leslie Tuttle,
for her enthusiastic help on this series.

Besides the fact that my sister-in-law
and good friend are both nurses,
I make no claim to being an expert on
nursing care. I had help in that department
from Corinne Aarsen, Diane Wierenga and
Ruth McNulty. Thank you as well to Steve Kondics,
Hera Angelo and Heather Toporowsky.

Prologue

"This is a fire-sale price, Simon, and you know it."

Simon Steele slipped his hands in the pockets of his leather jacket and lifted one shoulder in a shrug, negating the earnest comment from the real estate agent.

"Maybe," he drawled. "We both know the bank wants to dump this property, Blaine. Badly. The building needs major renovations to attract decent renters or owners." His quick glance took in the stained carpets and marked walls of the lobby before slanting the real estate agent a meaningful look and a smirk. "I'm prepared to offer thirty thousand less than the asking price. Firm." He ignored his partner, Oscar Delaney, who stood behind Blaine, shaking his head.

To his credit Blaine Nowicki never batted an eye. "Of course, I'll have to speak to my client on that and get back to you…"

"Phone them now and let's get this deal done," Simon interrupted, glancing at his watch. He didn't feel like playing out this fish any longer. He and Oscar had done their homework. They knew the situation at the bank and how long this particular apartment block had been on the market.

Long enough that Blaine's clients were willing to settle more quickly than he'd intimated.

"Simon, you're enough of a dealer to know that can't be done this quickly." Blaine fiddled with his tie as he favored Simon with an overly familiar smile that set Simon's teeth on edge. "This is a prime piece of property and worth far more than you're offering."

Simon held Blaine's determined gaze, his own features devoid of emotion. He lifted his hands, still in the pockets of his coat, signaling surrender. "Then, I'm history." He angled his chin in his partner's direction, "Let's go, Oscar. We've got a ferry to catch."

He turned and started walking away, measuring his tread so he looked like he was going quickly, yet giving Blaine enough time to protest before Simon hit the front doors of the lobby.

Oscar caught up to him, glancing sidelong at his partner with a frown. Simon gave him a warning shake of his head, then slowed fractionally as they approached the double doors.

For a moment he wondered if he had underestimated Blaine as he pulled his hand out of his pocket to grab the brass bar when…

"Wait," Blaine called out.

Simon allowed himself a moment of triumph, threw his partner an I-told-you-so glance, then forced the smirk off his face. When he turned to face Blaine, he was all business again.

"I'll call them right now," Blaine said, his cell phone in hand, his jacket flying open as he rushed over. "See what I can do for you." He punched in the numbers, frowning intently. Simon lifted his eyebrows at Oscar, who grinned back.

In ten minutes the papers were signed and Oscar and Simon were standing outside the building they had just purchased.

"I hope you know what you're doing," Oscar aid as they stood outside on the pavement, shivering in the damp that had rolled in.

Simon looked back at the five-story apartment block behind them. The first-story walls were pitted and marked, covered with graffiti. A few of the sliding glass doors were boarded up, but the rest of the building was sound.

"When you get back from vacation, we'll get some quotes on renovations," Simon said pulling his keys out of his pocket. "It's got a decent location. I'm sure once we get this thing fixed up, it will be full." He turned, squinting across the bay toward the hills of Vancouver Island now shrouded by the drizzle that had descended. He swung the keys around his finger. "It has a great view."

"When it's not raining," Oscar said, pulling his glasses off to clean them.

Simon grinned at his partner. "You sure you don't want to head south to the sun instead of camping with your wife's relatives? Why don't you come where I'm headed?"

"Right," Oscar said dryly, replacing his glasses. "I can see us already. Two overgrown teenagers on motorbikes heading down to the Baja." He pulled his coat closer, giving another shiver, moisture beading up on his dark blond hair. "Someone's got to be the mature, responsible one in this partnership."

Simon pulled a face. "Please, no bad language," he said with a laugh.

Oscar looked back at the apartment block. "You know, one of these days you should buy yourself a house instead of old apartment blocks and new businesses." He looked back at Simon, his expression serious.

"And start a family. Why not?" Simon flipped his keys once more, his tone sardonic. "One of those nice cozy groups of people you see on television commercials selling long-distance phone plans."

"Being on your own is no picnic," Oscar said as they headed toward a nearly deserted parking lot.

Simon stopped beside his bike and zipped up his leather coat with a decisive movement. "It's a whole lot easier than trying to work around other people's needs."

"Mr. Free Spirit personified," said Oscar with a rueful shake of his head. "One of these days you're going to get too old to keep running. Then you'll be panting and wheezing, wishing you had taken my advice and bought a nice house, found a nice girl and settled down."

"There is no such thing as a nice girl."

"Oh, c'mon. You just don't know where to look."

Simon pulled his helmet off his motorbike and dropped it on his head. "I suppose I could head out to your church. Scope out the girls there."

"Wouldn't hurt you to go once in a while anyhow." Oscar shivered again. "I gotta go. I've got a few things to do at the office before Angela and I leave town. She told her folks we'd be there before supper."

"See what I mean?" Simon said buckling up his helmet. "Family means schedule, expectations. Watch the clock. Stifling routine."

Oscar just looked at him, and Simon felt a flicker of reproach in his partner's gaze.

"Family means people who care too, Simon," Oscar said quietly. Simon looked away, snapping the top snap of his jacket, pulling on his gloves.

"Can't speak from personal experience on that," he said, forcing a light tone into his voice. He looked up at Oscar and shrugged the comment away. "I'll see you in a couple of weeks."

"Take care of yourself," Oscar said, hesitating as

if he would have liked to say more. Then he got in his vehicle and left.

Simon watched him go, his shoulders lifting in a sigh. He and Oscar had been partners for three years now. Oscar was a discreet sort of guy. He didn't pry, didn't ask a lot of questions and didn't intrude on Simon's personal life. Which is just what Simon wanted in a partner.

Simon liked things to be businesslike and at an arm's length distance from him. It made things a lot easier that way. The less people knew about you, the less of a hold they had over you. Strict access to information, he reminded himself as he pulled his leather pants over his now-damp jeans. That's what made his and Oscar's partnership work so well. Oscar only knew what he needed to know about Simon that pertained to how their partnership worked and vice versa.

Starting his bike, Simon turned onto the Island Highway and settled into a safe speed. He still had lots of time and would probably beat Oscar to the ferry.

As he drove his mind went back to his conversation with Oscar. He wished Oscar would lay off the broad hints about settling down. It was like an obsession with him.

Four years ago he and Oscar had met in a bar, had formed their loosely based partnership on the basis of a shared interest in the stock market and real estate.

Then Oscar got married, got religion and was now the sickeningly proud father of a little girl. Like a reformed smoker he was on Simon's case to follow suit.

Something Simon had no intention of doing. Oscar might look happy now, but people always let you down. That much Simon knew from personal experience.

And the many foster homes he'd been in after his mother had given him and his brother up for adoption when he was four. As far as he knew he had no other family. For a brief while, they had a loving father, Tom Steele—a widower who adopted them. When he died, he and Jake were moved, then moved again and finally split up.

Now Simon had no one.

He cut in front of a car and wove through the traffic, pushing the memories back into the recesses of his mind where they belonged. Living in the past did nothing for the present. And for the present, he was doing quite well, thank you very much. He and Oscar had a good business going. They made enough money that they could both take vacations when it suited them. And he could do pretty much as he pleased.

Yes, Simon thought as he gave the throttle another twist, he was doing very well indeed.

Chapter One

Heartbreak must be a regular occurrence here, Caitlin Severn thought, ignoring the elegantly dressed people in the hotel lobby who were politely ignoring her. She would have liked to walk through the lobby with her head up, but she couldn't. Her eyes prickled with unshed tears, and her nose was starting to run. It always did when she cried. She gave her eyes a careful wipe, and walked down the few steps toward the entrance.

When she got there, she stopped.

Perfect, she thought, staring out at the moisture dripping down the glass door. Her life was becoming more like a bad movie script with each passing moment. This unexpected drizzle was a dramatic touch. All she was missing was a soaring soundtrack.

She hugged herself, glancing over her shoulder

as if hoping that by doing so, Charles would come running up to her, pleading with her to change her mind. But he didn't.

The world carried on. Clichéd, but true. Nothing had stopped just because her own world had been rearranged.

Just ten minutes ago she had broken up with Charles Frost. Again. When Charles had made this date he'd said he had some special news. They'd been dating for three years, and she foolishly thought he was going to propose. Instead he told her about his promotion and subsequent move to Los Angeles.

In the moment when he lifted his glass of wine to her to toast his success, Caitlin was faced with something she knew she'd been avoiding.

Charles's career would always come before her.

Caitlin knew that this was not how she wanted to live her life.

So with a few succinct words, she broke up with him.

Caitlin took a step closer to the front doors and was grateful to see a row of cabs. With a last glance over her shoulder, she stepped out into the early evening drizzle.

She walked down the sidewalk, her high heels clicking on the wet pavement, moisture beading up on the fine fabric of the short, fitted dress she had chosen so carefully for this date and the "important news" Charles had to tell her.

Important to him, she thought with another sniff.

She hailed the first cab, then got in. She gave him quick directions to her home, then sat back, shivering with a combination of cold and reaction, thankful she had an escape.

As the driver pulled away from the front of the restaurant, she felt the first sob climb up her throat. She covered her mouth with her fist, but the hoarse cry slipped past her clenched hand into the quiet confines of the cab. One more got past her guard before Caitlin regained control. The cabbie didn't even look back.

She wouldn't cry, she thought as she defiantly swiped at her cheeks.

But Caitlin knew it was more than her breakup with Charles she grieved.

She watched out the window vaguely noting the buildings flowing by. She had lived in Nanaimo in Vancouver Island all her life and had never moved. It seemed as if her life had flowed along the same lines for the past twenty-eight years.

Twenty-eight and single again. Tonight, after their supper, she and Charles were to have gone to stay with his parents at their cabin on Pender Island for ten days.

And now...

Caitlin sighed. She wished she could skip the next few days and head back to work right away. The comforting steadiness of her work at the hospital would have taken her through the week, would have helped her get over the pain she felt. Now she didn't even have that.

Thankfully the driver was silent. The tires of the cab hissed over the wet pavement as a lethargy came over her. Reaction, she thought remembering all too easily the sight of Charles's impassive face as she delivered her ultimatum.

He just didn't care.

The entire evening stretched ahead of her, and she didn't feel like going home. She knew what would be waiting there. Her dear parents sitting in their usual chairs, drinking tea. Her sister Rachel would be curled up with her husband, Jonathon, on the couch, reading while soft music played on the stereo. Rachel, who had just told their parents she was expecting.

Caitlin had been jealous.

Caitlin shook her head at that thought. She was unable to put her finger precisely on why. It had much to do with the malaise she felt before she broke up with Charles. That her life was following the same path without any variation. She had the job she had trained for. She loved her work. But she still wanted someone in her life. Someone who needed her. She wanted to start her own family.

A blast from a motorcycle passing them made her jump. It zoomed ahead then slowed as the cab caught up. Puzzled, she watched, wondering what the motorcycle driver was doing. She found out as soon as the cab came up beside him again. In the bright streetlights, she saw the driver look sideways and, with a cheeky grin, wink at her.

Caitlin only stared back as he kept pace, still looking at her. He didn't look like anyone she would know. His well-shaped mouth had an insolent twist to it, his eyes shaded by his helmet seemed to laugh at her. Not her type.

Then he tossed a wave in her direction and with a twist of his wrist and a flick of his foot, was off again.

Caitlin shook her head at his audacity, watching as he wove expertly around the cab and the vehicle slightly ahead of them. Then a car swerved unexpectedly.

She heard a sickening *thud* as the car hit the biker. The bike wove once, then dropped, spinning in one direction while the driver shot off in another.

The cab driver slammed on the brakes and swerved to miss the driver.

"Stop," yelled Caitlin, leaning over the seat. "I'm a nurse. Stop."

The cabbie screeched to a halt twenty feet away from the driver, who now lay in a crumpled heap on the side of the road.

The car that caused the accident slowed, then sped away.

Caitlin's breath left her in a swoosh, her hands

shaking as she fumbled for the catch on the door. Finally she pushed it open and shot out of the cab. She ran to the driver who was moaning softly.

"Thank you Lord," she breathed at the sound. He was still alive.

Ignoring the expensive hose bought for this, her special night, the drizzle dripping down her neck, she dropped onto the wet pavement.

The cabbie came up behind her. "I called an ambulance, and the police," he said.

"Get me something to cover him with," she called out, as she automatically did her own assessment of the situation, drawing on her limited experience with emergencies. The man had a pulse, was breathing, albeit shallowly, and blood from a head injury ran in an ugly rivulet down his forehead. His leg was twisted at a grotesque angle. His leather coat was ripped.

Possible broken femur and spine injury, Caitlin thought, noting the angle of his leg. He's in big trouble. She knelt close to keep him from moving, her finger on his pulse as she counted and prayed.

The cab driver came back with an overcoat. "This is the best I could do. I got a first-aid kit, too."

Caitlin opened the kit as he spread the coat over the prone man. Right about now she regretted not having had more emergency training. In her ward at the hospital, she only got the patients from the operating room or emergency. All the critical care had been done by either paramedics or emergency room nurses.

Caitlin willed the ambulance to come, praying as she dug through the kit for a bandage to stop the bleeding from the most serious cut on his head. Her sore knees trembled with tension, she almost shivered in the damp weather, but she was afraid to shift position.

The man at her feet moaned, tried to roll over but was stopped by Caitlin's knees. He cried out, and his eyes flew open, staring straight up at Caitlin. "Hey, angel, you found me," he murmured, then his face twisted in pain.

Caitlin felt relief sluice through her in an icy wave even as she steeled herself against the sounds of his pain. Thankfully he was conscious. That meant no major head injury other than the cut on his temple. She carefully laid the pad on his head wound, applying pressure. "Can you feel your hands, your feet?"

"Yeah." She could tell that even that one word was an effort. "Feel too much."

"What's your name?"

"Doesn't matter…" He bit his lip. "Please stay."

"Are you allergic to anything?"

"No." He blinked, looking up at her, then arched his back and cried out again, grabbing her hand.

Caitlin winced at his strength. "Can you tell me where it hurts the most?"

"Everywhere." His words were slurred, and Caitlin feared he would lose consciousness after all.

"What's your name?" she repeated.

"You're a pain," he mumbled, still clinging to her hand. "Everything's a pain." He squeezed her hand, hard, moaning. "Who are you, angel?"

"I'm Caitlin. Tell me your name. Stay with me."

But though his hand clung tightly, he wouldn't answer.

"Please, Lord, keep him with us," she prayed aloud. "Keep him safe, help him. Please send that ambulance, now."

She watched him as she prayed. His eyes were shut, his lashes lying in dark spikes against his high cheekbones. His hair hung over his forehead, some of the strands caught in the trickle of blood from the wound on his forehead, curling in the damp.

He looked to be in his late twenties, well built, she reasoned from the weight of his body against her legs, the breadth of his shoulders. It made his vulnerability all the more heart-wrenching. Caitlin wanted to check his pulse, but his hand still held hers in a death grip.

"Can I do anything?" The cab driver hovered over her.

Caitlin glanced over her shoulder, feeling utterly helpless.

"Pray the ambulance comes quickly," she said,

shivering with reaction. The wind had picked up, chilling her.

In her peripheral vision she saw a few people coming out of their houses, some offering help. Someone even dropped a coat across her shoulders.

The victim's hand still clutched hers. Thankfully the flow of blood from his forehead eased, and Caitlin could put her finger on his pulse. It was weak, but then his grip loosened and his pulse slowed. Her prayers became more urgent as his eyes remained closed and beneath her trembling fingers she felt his life ebb away.

"Please, Lord, don't let him go. He's so young," she whispered, watching him. Nothing.

His breathing slowed.

Caitlin lifted his hand, clasped it against hers, her other hand still on his nonexistent pulse. *Please don't take him.*

Then, suddenly, his pulse returned, his hand tightened on hers.

His eyes fluttered open.

"You're still praying," he gasped.

"Yes, I am," Caitlin replied, relief turning her bones to rubber. He was still with her, he was still alive. "Thank you, Lord," she breathed.

She knew it wasn't over yet. His broken femur and the accompanying loss of blood were life threatening.

But she was reassured by the solid answer she received—a touch of God's hand on the situation.

"You're wasting your time praying," he said, his teeth clenched against the pain.

"No, I'm not," Caitlin whispered, shaky with reaction.

Then came the welcome wail of an ambulance's sirens and its blue and red lights, flashing through the gathering dusk.

"What happened?" A paramedic ran up to Caitlin while the driver jumped out and pulled the stretcher out of the back.

"Motorcycle accident." As relief weakened her legs, she forced herself to stay calm, to be the professional nurse she was, relating what she had seen of the accident and how she'd treated his injuries. The police could deal with the driver of the car. She was more concerned about her patient. As the older of the paramedics immediately positioned himself at the victim's head, stabilizing it, she said, "I'm a nurse so tell me what to do."

"Just step back for now, ma'am."

She quickly got up and out of the way, her knees aching. She drew the stranger's coat around her, shivering against the chill wind.

The paramedic at the victim's head had his knees on either side, stabilizing him as he checked his breathing, the pulse at his throat. "Give me O2, ten liters, non-rebreather," he called out to his partner as he lifted the victim's eyelids.

"He's conscious. Superficial head injury," the young paramedic said as he started an IV.

"I need a C collar, large."

"Spine seems okay, no internal injuries so far. Fracture of right femur. Both arms, okay. Possible sprain."

"Got the fracture stabilized."

"Let's get him on the board."

The older paramedic at his head looked up at Caitlin. "We'll need your help, now, ma'am."

She nodded, and positioned herself. "Watch for that fracture," she couldn't help saying.

"On three." They rolled him onto the board, the paramedic still holding his head. With quick, efficient movements they had the victim strapped in, stabilizing him. Someone handed her her purse while she watched. The paramedics placed foam on either side of his head, taped the foam in, strapped the spine board on the stretcher and slid him into the ambulance, headfirst. It was all done with a calm efficiency that drew Caitlin along, comforting her. Routine she understood. What she didn't understand was her reluctance to let this man go.

"I'm coming," Caitlin decided suddenly. She handed the coat to someone and scooted into the ambulance before it sped away.

Caitlin's head ached in the overly bright lights of the ambulance's interior as she braced herself against the movement. She sat down on the long bench beside the stretcher. Vaguely she heard the driver on the radio, "Patch me into the hospital…"

Caitlin felt as if her breath still had to catch up to her.

The older paramedic switched the oxygen to a fixture in the wall of the ambulance.

"What can I do?" she asked, reaction setting in. She was a nurse, and she needed to be busy.

"Here's a blood pressure cuff and stethoscope. Get me a set of vitals." He smiled at her as he handed her the equipment. "I'm Stan."

"I'm Caitlin." She unrolled the cuff and stuck the stethoscope in her ears.

"Hey, guy, you with me?" Stan asked the victim while he did a head-to-toe check again, opening the patient's leather jacket and his shirt to check his chest and stomach. "What's his name?" he asked Caitlin, as he worked.

"I don't know," Caitlin looked up at Stan, then down at the patient. His face was hidden by the oxygen mask, his eyes shut. His skin had a waxy pallor that concerned her.

The driver called back, "Is he awake?"

"Yes, but poor response. He's a little shocky," said Stan, as he steadied himself in the moving ambulance.

"Vitals are b.p. 118 on 76, pulse 116, respirations 24" Caitlin told him, pulling the stethoscope out of her ears.

Stan nodded as he pressed on the patient's sternum. The ambulance swayed around a corner and then with a short wail of sirens, came to a stop.

"Let's go Caitlin," Stan said as he pulled a blanket over the patient. The door swung open, and Caitlin grabbed the coat and purse, exiting with the stretcher into a murmur of voices.

She strode alongside the stretcher as they entered the warmth and light of the hospital, watching the unknown man. His eyes flickered open, looked wildly around.

Caitlin lightly touched his face and he homed in on her. He blinked, and through the oxygen mask she saw his lips move. He lifted his hand toward her, then with a grimace of pain, faded away again.

Stan gave the triage nurse and doctor a quick rundown of what he knew and what they had done.

"Put him in the trauma room," she said and Caitlin stood back while they wheeled the stranger down the hall and away from her.

It was over, but she still couldn't walk away.

Caitlin felt the noise and heat press in on her aching head. For a brief moment, she felt all alone in a room full of people caught up in their own pains and sorrows.

She found an empty chair and sat on the edge, bunching her purse on her lap. Unbelievably the delicate shawl was still wound around her shoulder but her nylons sported a large hole in one knee, she noted with a disoriented feeling.

As an orthopedic nurse she rarely saw death. When she did, it was in a hospital setting where there was immediate help. Routine. What she had seen tonight was raw and powerful—a potent reminder of how fragile life was.

She heard a measured tread and looked up as the paramedic named Stan stood in front of her.

"Caitlin, you okay?"

"Yeah, I'm fine." She smiled weakly up at him, surprised he remembered her name. "How is he?"

"They've got him stabilized. They're going to get him into OR right away. He's been asking for you by name. Do you know him?"

"No. I gave my name when I was trying to find out about him." Caitlin frowned, surprised this man who must be in a tremendous amount of pain would remember her. "Can I see him?"

"He's headed for the operation room. But if you wait, you might catch a glimpse of him as he's wheeled by."

Caitlin got up, her knees still trembling. She followed Stan down the hallway, her shoes clicking loudly on the floor. "Just wait here," he said. "I've got to go now. Take care, Caitlin."

Nodding, Caitlin waited until the curtain on the cubicle was pushed aside and the stretcher wheeled out.

Caitlin caught up to the stretcher, walking quickly alongside it.

"Are you Caitlin?" the nurse pushing the stretcher asked.

"Yes," Caitlin replied quietly, looking down at the stranger, his face still obscured by the oxygen mask. His eyes were open, focused intently on her, his hair still matted with blood. Caitlin couldn't stop staring at him. His high cheekbones and full mouth gave his features a fascinating appeal.

He reached out for her and once again, Caitlin caught his hand. "You'll be okay," she said as they hurried down the hallway. "I'll be praying for you. You're in good hands."

"I am now," he said, his voice muffled by the oxygen mask, his hand squeezing hers.

Chapter Two

This is ridiculous, Caitlin thought as she strode down the hallway to her own unit. You don't know anything about that motorcycle victim. He's not your concern. For the past two hours she had wandered around the emergency department then gone for coffee. It was now nine-thirty, and she'd decided to see this through to the end and go up to the ward where the unknown man would be taken after surgery.

It was the best way she knew of avoiding home and facing the questions of her family when she showed up there. It seemed the only logical thing to do.

Sort of logical, she thought, ignoring her self-doubts over this impulsive, un-Caitlin-like behavior.

She approached the desk of the ward she had been working at since she graduated from nursing school. It was as familiar to her as her own street.

And so was the face of the nurse at the desk.

"Hey, Caitlin, what are you doing here?" Danielle asked, leaning her elbows on the desk, fully prepared to chat. "Thought you and Charles had a date?"

"We did. I cut it short." She knew she had taken a chance coming up here instead of going home. Danielle Jones and Caitlin had been friends since nursing school. Danielle knew all Caitlin's secrets. But coming to her ward seemed the less painful of two evils. "You busy?"

"Steady. Got a guy coming up from OR in a while. Motorcycle accident."

Caitlin felt a guilty flush climb up her cheeks. "I know," she said. "I saw it happen."

Danielle frowned, shaking her head. "That must have been horrible. That why you cut your date with Charles short?" She glanced over Caitlin's dress. "By the way you look gorgeous, sweetie. That bronze dress sets off your blond hair just perfectly."

"Thanks," Caitlin said ignoring her first question. She walked around the desk, glancing at the assignment board. "Mrs. Johnson's been discharged over the weekend?"

"She had a miraculous recovery when her reluctant daughter said she would come to the house to help." Danielle picked up a pen, made a few more notes on a chart then looked back up at Caitlin. "So, how is the very handsome Charles Frost?"

Caitlin felt a pain clutch her chest at the mention

of her boyfriend's name. Ex-boyfriend she reminded herself. "He got a promotion," she murmured, flipping through some papers on the desk, deliberately avoiding the reality of what she had done.

"Wow, you must be pleased."

"As punch." Caitlin stopped her pointless fiddling.

"You don't sound pleased." Danielle tapped the pencil on the desk. "Sit down. I've got time."

Caitlin was just about to say no, but Danielle looked concerned and she needed a sympathetic ear. Who better than her best friend? So she sat down, unwinding her shawl from her neck.

Danielle reached over and laid a gentle hand on her friend's shoulder. "What's wrong, Caitlin?"

She opted for the direct approach and told her the day's events.

"I broke up with Charles tonight," she said, her tone deliberate.

"What?"

"He said he had good news." Caitlin plowed on, ignoring Danielle's expression of utter surprise. "Unfortunately like an optimistic idiot, I thought he meant…" her voice trailed off as she took a quick breath, embarrassed.

"He was going to propose." Danielle finished off the sentence.

"I should have known," Caitlin said angrily, crushing the scarf on her lap. She loosed it, carefully smoothing it out again, glancing up at her friend. "The past few months we've been drifting apart, but I kept hoping things would change for both of us," she said with a wry laugh.

"Well then it's a good thing you broke up with him. If I find out in a couple of dates this isn't the kind of guy I want to spend the rest of my life with, *phwwt...*" Danielle made a dismissive gesture with one hand. "Out he goes. Companionship I can get from my friends and pets. Hanging on is a waste of time."

And how much time hadn't she wasted, Caitlin thought, considering the three years of dating Charles.

"I thought Charles and I were headed in that direction, but I guessed wrong." Caitlin shook her head, winding the scarf around her hands. "Can you believe I was that dumb?" She clenched her fists, shaking her head.

"Well, at the risk of sounding like a cliché, I'm sure you'll get over it. I mean Charles is a nice guy, he's good-looking, he's ambitious, but..." Danielle lifted her hands as if in surrender. "I just don't sense a real spark between you two."

Caitlin said nothing at that, knowing that, as usual, her friend had put her finger directly on Caitlin's own malaise concerning the relationship.

Before she could formulate an answer, the recovery room called to say they were sending up the accident victim.

Caitlin glanced at the clock. There was no avoiding it, she had to go home sooner or later. "Well, I'm history," she said, winding the scarf around her shoulders and picking up her purse.

"I should make sure the room is ready for our new admission," Danielle conceded, getting up. "Will I see you before you fly down to visit your sister Evelyn and her new baby?"

Caitlin nodded, wondering how she'd fill the ten days before she left for Portland. "Yeah. I'll need something to do besides sit and watch my mother eagerly knitting baby booties. Rachel's expecting, too!"

Danielle touched her arm as if sensing Caitlin's yearning for her own family. "You want me to call a cab?"

"I'll get one myself. Thanks." Caitlin smiled at her friend. Danielle gave her a quick hug and then left.

Caitlin sighed lightly, and turned to go. But when the elevator door swooshed open, a stretcher was wheeled into the ward. The motorcyclist.

Caitlin stopped beside the stretcher, taking another look at the patient lying there. A fine net held his hair back, exposing his strong features. A dressing covered the gash on his forehead.

The patient moaned once, his eyes fluttered open and homed in on hers. He blinked, tried to lift his head and then closed his eyes again.

But once again his hand reached out toward her and once again, Caitlin took a step closer and took it in hers. He squeezed it lightly. "Angel," he whispered, the word coming out in a sigh. "Don't go."

And Caitlin knew she was staying.

Someone was talking to him. The words came slowly, echoing down a long, dark corridor. Simon tried to catch them but he couldn't move, couldn't focus on what the voice said.

More words and sounds coming closer, sharper. Then, finally, "He's coming around." The words pierced the haze of darkness holding him captive.

"Can you hear me?" the voice continued.

Why was it so much work to talk, to do something as simple as lift his eyelids?

He struggled and as awareness dawned so did the pain. It pressed down on him, heavy, overwhelming, taking over his slowly awakening senses.

He moaned, the sound forced out of him by the extent of an agony he couldn't pinpoint. Where was he?

He tried to focus, to comprehend. It was so much work. A face swam into his vision and he strained to see it better. He blinked hard, willing his eyes to function.

Finally the blurred edges coalesced. He recognized his angel of mercy, her soft green eyes like a refreshing drink.

He called out as he closed his eyes, fighting a fresh wave of pain. Cool fingers slipped through his. With another effort, he clung to her as if to a lifeline.

More movement as he felt himself being lifted, then a surge of pain.

He dug his head back into the pillow as he rode it out. It slowly eased, but he kept his eyes shut as he breathed through the last bit.

"Where are you?" he panted. "Angel."

"I'm here." She touched his face lightly. "Just try to rest now," she said, fussing over the blanket, tucking it around his chest. She straightened, pulled up a chair and sat down beside him.

He felt himself drifting off again. He didn't want to go, didn't like the feeling but couldn't stop it.

Unaware of how much time had passed, he felt himself drifting, heard voices far away.

Then increasing agony pulled him up into awareness. He fought it, preferring the blessed relief of the darkness, the not knowing to the perception of deep aching overlaid with sharp pain.

"Hi, there." A soft voice beside him made him turn his head toward the gentle sound. "How are you doing?"

He forced his eyes open and there she was again. The face he'd been seeing since this all started. Every time he opened his eyes, she was there.

A name drifted out of another part of his memory, attaching itself to her serene beauty. Caitlin.

"It hurts," was all he could say when he wanted to say so much more. *Who are you? Why are you always here?*

"Do you want something for the pain?" she asked, leaning forward. Her hand was a light touch on his forehead, a connection with reality.

"Please," he gasped. Anything to escape this agony, he thought at the same time resenting his vulnerability. He closed his eyes, searching for some bit of memory to explain what had happened to him. The only thing he could remember was seeing her again and again.

Then he felt that same gentling hand at the back of his neck. "Here," she said quietly. "Open your mouth." He obeyed and she placed something on his tongue. He opened his eyes again, seeking hers as she held a cup of tepid water to his lips. He swallowed, thankful for the moisture then lay back, watching as she set the cup on the table and sat down again.

"What's your name?" she asked, leaning forward, taking his hand in hers.

"Why do you want to know?" he mumbled, pain pressing his eyes closed.

"So I know who I'm praying for," she said quietly, squeezing his hand lightly.

"Waste of time," he said.

"Please. I want to know who you are."

Light from the hallway, muted by the curtain around him shone on her delicate features. What was she doing here and why did she want to know his name?

The questions grew fuzzy, his need to find answers receding as the pill took effect.

She squeezed his hand again. "Don't drift off on me without telling me your name."

He sensed she wasn't going to stop. He didn't like the frustration that edged her voice and decided, reluctantly, to grant her request. "My name is Simon."

That made her smile and he was glad.

"Thanks for being here," he said, squeezing her hand back. Then blessed unconsciousness brought him ease.

Again, he was unaware of the passage of time, aware only that each time he came up from the darkness, she was there, offering what comfort she could.

Once he woke to find her sleeping, her head pillowed on the bed, her face buried in her arms. The room was dark. He felt unaccountably bereft, alone. He didn't want to disturb her, but felt an urgent need to connect, to touch.

Her hair lay in tangled disarray close to his hand. He reached out and touched it, marveling at its softness, wondering again who she was and why she had stayed with him.

But his mind didn't have much room for wondering. It was taken up by a throbbing ache in his legs, arms, chest.

"Caitlin," he whispered, then he drifted off again.

Chapter Three

Caitlin didn't want to think what she was doing here. One o'clock in the morning was no time to figure out where else to go.

A moan from the bed made her turn. She'd only meant to catch a few winks when she laid her head on the bed, but had, instead, slept a couple of hours. She got up, the floor cool under her feet.

"Caitlin." Simon's voice was a harsh whisper. "My throat's sore."

It still gave her a start to hear him speak her name. She turned to see him looking at her, his eyes glinting in the refracted light coming from outside. For a moment she held his gaze, wondering again why she stayed, why he seemed to want her with him.

With a shake of her head she dismissed the thoughts. Walking to his side, she poured him some water, lifted his head and let him take a drink. He swallowed with difficulty and then laid his head back. "Your throat is sore from a tube that gets put down your throat during surgery," she explained. "Your chest will be sore, too."

"What happened to me?"

Caitlin relived the shock of the accident. She had been so close to it all.

"Caitlin?" he asked again. "Tell me."

"You were in a motorbike accident. You've sustained some very serious injuries."

"How serious?" he asked, closing his eyes and drawing in a breath.

"You've a fractured femur, a bruised pelvis and bruises that I'm sure you're beginning to feel."

"How did it happen?"

"I didn't see all of it. A car hit you, and your bike went down on top of you." She took a slow, deep breath, seeing the accident again. She'd explained what happened to other patients many times before, but never had the picture of the events been so indelibly printed in her mind. Never had she seen a cocky smile replaced by a grimace of pain, a man full of self-confidence in one moment, thrown like a rag doll across the pavement in the next. She wondered if she would ever forget it.

"You helped me."

Caitlin laughed a short laugh. "I did very little."

"You stopped." He turned his head, his hand reaching out to her. Caitlin wanted to pretend she didn't see it. Wanted to break the tenuous connection they had developed by her being by his side. One look at his eyes narrowed with pain, the lines along his full mouth and she couldn't stop herself from placing her hand in his. "You're here now," he said, his voice hoarse as he tightly grasped her hand. "Why?"

Because I don't know where else to go right now? Because, unlike my ex-boyfriend, you needed me?

But as she looked at him, she knew it was more.

Caitlin kept her replies to herself and only squeezed his hand a little harder. "Doesn't matter. Just try to rest."

He took a slow breath, his eyes drifting shut. "Stay with me a little longer, Caitlin?"

"I'll be here," she said softly. "Now, don't talk anymore."

He lifted one corner of his mouth. A careful smile. Then she felt his fingers loosen their grip on hers but not enough to let go.

With a sigh, she pulled the chair up closer and tried to get some more sleep.

Caitlin woke a few hours later, blinking in the brightness of the room. The curtains behind her only muted the morning light pouring in over her shoulder.

Her one arm was asleep, her hand still anchored in Simon's. Carefully, she pulled it free. His fingers fluttered a moment as if seeking hers, and Caitlin thought he would waken.

But he slept on, his breathing heavy.

Caitlin stretched her hand in front of her, wincing at the harsh prickling. She yawned and pulled a face at the stale taste in her mouth.

She got up, grabbing the arm of the chair as her one leg gave way under her. She had slept in an awkward position, her arms on the bed.

Sometime in the night she had kicked off her shoes. She saw one beside the chair, the other had been pushed under the bed.

Her stomach was empty, a grim reminder of her missed supper last night. Her neck was stiff, her shoulders sore and her mouth felt fuzzy.

Last night she had been angry and her impetuous decision to come here wasn't made with a rational mind and now she was paying for it.

She bit back a sigh as the events of last night came back with the cold clarity that accompanies the sharp light of morning.

Charles and she had broken up, and this time she knew it was for good. She knew she didn't want to go back to the half limbo that had been their relationship the past while.

Caitlin glanced at Simon. His face was drawn, his hair was caked with blood at the temple. The sight of him reaching out to her, pleading for her to stay had struck the very spot Charles had wounded with his lack of caring. This man, this total stranger, made her feel needed, and after last night it was what drew her toward him.

But now, it was morning. The night was over and she had to get home and…

Caitlin bit her lip, thinking of telling her parents and her sister. Her family who all thought the world of Charles and who wanted so badly for Charles and Caitlin to come to a stronger commitment. Her family to whom finding someone and marrying was the natural progression of events. Her older sister was married and had just had her third child. Her younger sister was married and expecting her first. Even her unreliable brother was married, living off in the east who knew where.

But he's married, Caitlin thought wryly. And I'm not.

She glanced again at the man on the bed. He'd had a restless night and Danielle was thankful for Caitlin's presence. They had two more admissions and were running off their feet.

After her brief nap she'd given him his pain medication, adjusted his leg, keeping it elevated to avoid blood clots. She tried to talk to him when he was lucid, tried to ask him questions about his relatives, his family. They would need to be notified. But he'd said nothing.

There had to be someone who would need to

know about him, she figured. Parents, brother, sister. Maybe a girlfriend?

"What do you care?" Caitlin admonished herself, reaching down and pulling her other shoe out from under the bed. "You won't be back here." She slipped her shoes on, thinking of her much anticipated vacation.

"And what are you going to do about that?" she asked herself, stretching once again.

She glanced at her watch, groaning at the time. Six o'clock in the morning. Her parents would still be sleeping, and she badly wanted to change.

"Hi there."

Caitlin turned at the sound of the sleep-roughened voice. Simon was watching her, and she wondered how long he had been awake, listening to her babble to herself.

"Hi, yourself," she said, crossing her arms across her stomach as she walked to the side of the bed. He looked pale, his eyes still dull with pain. "How are you doing?"

"Horrible. I feel like I've been hit by a train." He tried to lick his lips. "My mouth feels like I've been on an all-nighter."

"In a way, you have," Caitlin replied. "Want some ice water?"

"Sounds wonderful," his voice drifted off on the last syllable and Caitlin guessed he was in pain again.

"Do you want some painkillers with that?"

"I don't know," he whispered, his teeth clenched. "I hate the way they make me feel."

"I'm sure it can't be worse than the way that plate in your leg makes you feel?"

"What?" Simon blinked, tried to raise his head and then fell back with a grimace. "What are you talking about?"

"Drink first," she ordered, raising his head and placing the cup against his lips.

He took a long drink and then lay back. "Now tell me," he demanded.

"Do you remember what I told you about the accident?"

He nodded.

"They had to fix the fracture with a metal plate and screws. The surgeon will be doing his rounds later on and he can tell you exactly what he did to your leg."

"Where's my bike?"

"That I can't tell you. We'll be in contact with the police later on. They can let us know where it is and how badly it was damaged."

"What about the other guy?"

"The one who hit you?"

Simon only nodded, his eyes shut again.

"It was hit-and-run. Like I said, I saw it, but didn't get a clear view of the license plate. I'll have to tell the police what I know, and I'm sorry I can't tell you more."

Simon opened his eyes, zeroing in on her. "Why did you stay with me all night?"

Caitlin pulled her hand back, feeling the impact of his direct gaze. She still wasn't able to analyze why she had done it. "I saw the accident. I came with you in the ambulance. I stayed because the night staff was running off their feet…."

"Thanks," he whispered, his perfectly shaped mouth curving up in a smile. He closed his eyes again and was gone.

Caitlin drew in a shaky breath, trying to dispel the odd feeling his smile gave her. A feeling much different from any that Charles's smiles had created.

Rebound, she reminded herself with disgust. That and the ego-building feeling of being wanted by a man she knew had an earthy appeal most women would notice.

"So you can't leave earlier for Evelyn's place, what else are you going to do?" Rachel bent over and picked up a rock, angling her hand. With a flick of her wrist she tossed it out, and it skipped across the quiet water of Piper's Lagoon.

"I don't know. I sure don't feel like hanging around Nanaimo for ten days, but I don't have the energy to make other plans." Caitlin shoved her hands deeper into the pockets of her jean jacket, her feet scuffing through the shale and rock of the beach, retracing steps they had taken so often in their youth.

Caitlin needed to get out and away from her mother's sympathetic glances, her sorrowing looks. Her mother really liked Charles and had so hoped he would someday be her son-in-law.

Well those hopes were dashed as surely as the shells she was even now crunching under her feet.

"Maybe you should go away. Take a trip with all that money you've got saved up."

"I don't know where I'd want to go. And I don't feel like traveling alone."

"Yeah, I know what you mean." Rachel slipped her arm around her sister's waist. "I just don't like seeing you like this, so lost and forlorn."

"I'm not forlorn," Caitlin said with a note of disgust in her voice. "I'm probably more ticked than anything. Going back to him and then breaking up with him." Caitlin stopped at a driftwood log and lowered herself to the sand, leaning against the log. The September air was quiet, unusually still. A white gull wheeled above them, sending out a shrill, haunting cry. The afternoon sun shimmered on the water. It was as if the entire world had slowed down.

"You look tired."

Caitlin shrugged. She had told her family about spending the night at the hospital, but not why. Sitting at Simon's bedside seemed quixotic in the harsh light of the day. She came home just before her family came back from church, giving her time to shower and change. It also gave her time for personal devotions, and a chance to question God about the events of the past twenty-four hours.

"What about going back to work?" Rachel sat down beside her, sifting her hands through the coarse sand, tilting her face to the sun.

"I would dearly love to, but unfortunately it's not an option." Caitlin settled farther down on the log, squinting against the sun to the mountains of the mainland beyond. Mountains as familiar as the wallpaper of her own bedroom. She and Rebecca spent hours here. It was a short bike ride from their parent's home. In the summer they swam here, on cooler days they walked along the beach, exploring, planning, dreaming. "All the shifts are planned out. Much as I'd love to get back to work, I'd throw a huge monkey wrench in the whole business if I tried to get back into it right now." She pushed her hand into the sun-warmed sand, reaching down to the cooler layer below.

"Well, you have to make some plans."

Caitlin wrinkled her nose and laid her head back against the log, letting the sun warm her face. "I don't have to make any plans. I've spent three years working around Charles's schedule, and I think the next week and a half will be a good opportunity for me to figure out my own life."

"Have you ever thought about moving out of Mom and Dad's house?"

Caitlin squinted across the bay again, looking but not seeing. Right now she didn't want to make any decision more strenuous than whether she should get up and keep walking or stay leaning against this log while her behind got slowly colder. "I should," she said. "It's just too easy at home. Mom takes care of me, and I don't have to think about anything."

"Well, someday you'll find somebody. Someone you can care for." Rachel reached over and stroked her shoulder, trying to comfort Caitlin.

"I suppose I will," Caitlin said stifling a sigh. She didn't know if she wanted to invest her emotions in another relationship. It seemed a lot of work for little reward. She pushed herself up, brushing the cool, damp sand off her pants and giving her sister a hand, pulled her up. "I guess I'll just have to wait for someone to come and sweep me off my feet."

"Charles will regret this, you know."

Caitlin pursed her lips, nodding absently at her sister's confident proclamation.

"I think he was just taking you for granted. He's probably just afraid of commitment."

"He seems pretty committed to his job," Caitlin said dryly. "And if he can't give me that same kind of commitment, then I'm really wasting my time."

"Maybe breaking up with him will show him that you're serious. It will be a wake-up call for him."

Rachel smiled at her sister in encouragement. "You just wait. He'll be calling you by the end of the week, begging you to come back."

"We've done this break-up-and-begging thing before. I wouldn't take him, Rachel," Caitlin said firmly, her hands bunched in the pockets of her jean jacket.

"What?" Rachel punched her sister on the shoulder. "Of course you would. Charles is such a great guy."

Caitlin looked down at some shells, kicking them up and watching them fall. "He may be great, but I don't know if I've had any passionate feelings for him." She angled a questioning glance at her sister. "Surely that should be part of a relationship."

"I still can't believe you're saying this."

"I can. Amazing what a few different events can do to change your perspective on life."

"Like what?"

Caitlin stopped and turned to face her sister. "Yesterday you told me you were expecting. Yesterday I saw a man almost get killed. I realized how precious life is and how much of mine I've wasted waiting to see if Charles could squeeze me into his agenda."

"What?" Rachel said, frowning. "What do you mean about a man getting killed? You never said anything about that."

Caitlin held her sister's puzzled gaze and then

turned away, walking a little quicker. "It happened after I broke up with Charles. Some guy on a motor-bike." His name is Simon, her inner voice taunted her. You stayed with him, all night. He's more than "some guy." "It was pretty traumatic and it shook me up." she continued, ignoring the insidious thoughts. "He was afraid and wanted me to stay with him. So I did. That's why I was home so late."

"Wow, Caity. That was nice of you."

Caitlin was reassured by the tone of her sister's voice, by her use of an innocuous word like *nice.* It told her that what she had done was kindness, nothing more. It had nothing to do with emptiness and being needed. Nothing to do with eyes that de-manded and a mouth that promised.

Chapter Four

"You didn't tell me Eva was working evenings." Caitlin pulled a face at the timesheet in front of her. Danielle had called her earlier in the day to offer her the shift for a nurse who'd wanted to take the week off but hadn't been able to because of Caitlin's pending vacation with Charles.

Danielle gave her friend a light punch on the shoulder. "Beggars can't be choosers, my dear. If it's any comfort, I'll be in the last two days of the rotation. We can gossip together." A light blinked on above the doorway across from the nurse's station and Danielle looked up with a frown. "There goes that Simon again," she grumbled. "Had that student nurse, Tina, all in a dither this morning."

"Do you want me to go?" Caitlin offered.

"Sure. Just don't let him get to you!" warned her friend.

Caitlin only smiled. "I think I'm okay in that department," she said as she walked into his room. She knew she wouldn't be succumbing to any male charms for a while.

"Took you long enough," Simon grumbled as she walked to the foot of his bed. As he glanced at her he frowned, then his hazel eyes brightened "Well, hi there, angel," he said a slow smile curving his lips, his gravelly voice softening. "You came back to see me."

Caitlin could see how this man could get a young woman flustered. With just a smile, a shifting of his features, he changed from harsh to appealing. "I just came on the ward to see when I'm working again," she said, walking over to his side. "Danielle's busy. Did you want some water?" She poured him a cup.

"You work here?" He shifted as he reached for the cup, his smile disappearing in a grimace of pain.

"Yes, I do. I'm on vacation now though, but I'll be back tomorrow."

"Really?" He tried to smile again, but he squeezed his eyes shut and took a few slow breaths, fighting the agony Caitlin knew he must be suffering.

"Do you want a painkiller?" she asked quietly, taking the cup out of his trembling hands.

He shook his head once, quickly. "No," he gasped, "I'm okay."

Caitlin watched him battling the pain, his head

pressed back against the pillow, his fists clenched at his sides.

"You don't have to suffer like this," she said, touching his shoulder lightly. "You don't have to be so tough."

Simon took a few more quick breaths, then slowly exhaled, his eyes opening. "Maybe not," he said with a sigh. "I hate feeling out of control."

"Better than feeling like that motorbike landed on you all over again," Caitlin said dryly, setting the cup down on the table.

"Maybe," he whispered, beads of sweat glistening on his forehead.

"When's the last time you had something?" she asked, folding her arms across her chest.

"I don't know."

"I'm going to check."

He opened his eyes. "You coming back?"

Caitlin paused. His brusque question held a faint note of entreaty at odds with his character. Their eyes met, held, and for a heartbeat Caitlin felt the same emotion he had created in her the night of his accident.

He needed her.

Caitlin forced herself to look away, to break the tenuous connection.

Don't be ridiculous she reprimanded herself as she walked out of the room and over to the desk. He's just doing what comes naturally. Flirting.

"So, what did the old bear want now?" Danielle asked, looking up from her paperwork.

"When was the last time he had a painkiller?"

Danielle reached over and pulled up Simon's chart, shaking her head. "If you want to give him something, I wish you luck. He won't take anything unless he's just about dead from pain. I've been tempted to slip him something in his IV." She flipped through the papers. "Here. About five hours ago. He's got to be hurting now."

"He is."

Danielle nodded. "Dr. Hall changed the order this morning. He's got him on a stronger medication. I'll get him something. Maybe between the two of us we can get it in him." Danielle left and Caitlin walked back to the room.

Simon lay still, his arms at his sides, his eyes closed.

"Is that you, angel?" he asked, his voice quiet.

"It's Caitlin, not angel."

He carefully opened his eyes, zeroing in on her immediately. "When I first saw you, I thought you were an angel, then you saved my life."

"I didn't save your life, either," Caitlin said matter-of-factly.

"I felt myself slipping away, going down into darkness, I knew I was going…." He stopped, took a deep breath at the effort of talking. "But you pulled me back." He smiled wanly at her. "How did you do it?"

Caitlin held his gaze. "I prayed."

"Sure."

"Your heartbeat was weakening, almost nonexistent," she replied, ignoring the sarcasm in his voice. "I was praying and then it came back. Simple as that."

Simon shook his head, closing his eyes again. "I don't believe you." He took another breath and Caitlin could tell from the lines around his mouth he was really hurting.

Danielle came in the room with a med cup. "Here we are," she said, handing it to Caitlin. "See if you can get that in him." She looked back at Simon. "I couldn't connect with Oscar, Simon. Do you want me to try again?"

"No," he replied tightly. "He's camping. I forgot."

"I'm going on a break now, Caitlin. I'll be back in about twenty minutes to check his dressings."

Danielle left and Caitlin set the small paper cup on the bedside table. "Are you going to take this?"

Simon opened his eyes again. "What are you going to do if I don't?" he said forcing a wry smile. "Pray again?"

"That, and put something in your IV, or give you a needle. Either of those will really knock you out." Caitlin picked up the med cup and his glass of water. "This is a better alternative."

"Isn't that against my human rights?"

"Hospitals are not a democracy," she said shaking her head at his obtuseness.

"Total dictatorship," he said with a short laugh. He reached up and took the cup. He tipped the pill into his mouth and then grimaced. "This place sounds like my old foster home."

He handed Caitlin the paper cup and lay back again. His comment about foster homes piqued Caitlin's curiosity. "You know, I never did find out your last name," she said pulling up a chair.

"Read my chart," he said obliquely. He glanced sidelong at Caitlin. "You settling in for a heart-to-heart chat?"

"Hardly," Caitlin said. "Just making sure you didn't put that pill under your tongue so you can spit it out later. If I sit here long enough it will dissolve."

"Do you want me to open my mouth so you can check?"

"That will be fine." She watched him a moment, knowing she should leave, but curiously unwilling to.

"So, where are you from?" she asked, leaning back in the chair, lightly tapping her fingers on the armrests.

Simon looked away, his hazel eyes, narrowing. "Does it matter? Knowing that won't change anything." He sounded testy, angry.

Caitlin stopped tapping and tilted her head to one side, studying him. "It makes you more of an individual. Tells me something about you."

Simon curved his mouth into a smile but it lacked the warmth and appeal of the smile he favored her with a few moments. "I'm from nowhere, and I don't have a family." The statement was made without emotion, without any attempt to garner pity from the listener.

"What about Oscar Delaney?"

"He's my partner."

"You also said something about a foster home...."

Simon glanced sidelong at Caitlin, his eyes hard. "I think you better go now," he said firmly.

Caitlin held his gaze until he looked away. He was breathing quickly, fighting the agony she knew must be coursing through his body, confusing him and making him short-tempered. She got up and carefully pushed the chair back against the wall under the window, feeling slightly frustrated herself and wondering why she should care. "Do you want me to pull the curtains?" she asked, reverting to her role as a nurse and professional.

He shook his head, his eyes drifting shut again. Caitlin waited a moment, watching as his mouth relaxed, the frown eased from his forehead. The medication was kicking in, she thought. He looked more peaceful now, and Caitlin couldn't deny his appeal.

Wavy hair that fell over his forehead, hiding the cut, high cheekbones, a mouth that could curl up in disdain and yet, now that he was asleep, show a softness she knew he wouldn't want to show.

She was still surprised that no one had come to see him, that no one missed him.

Then again, she wondered why she should care. In spite of his good looks, he was a patient. She was a nurse.

"But I need this information, Mr. Steele." The young nurse looked down at the clipboard she was carrying.

Simon looked up at the woman hovering at his bedside, wishing she would go. He hadn't slept much last night, his leg was throbbing, his arm and the top of his leg felt as if they were on fire, and he was tired of feeling woozy from the medication he was on. And now he had an ambitious nurse standing by his bed pumping him for information. He still hadn't been able to connect with Oscar and he was feeling hemmed in and testy.

"I want you to leave me alone. You've got all the information you need to have. My insurance number, legal name, allergies and previous medical history, as far as I know."

"But we need an emergency contact number and…"

"Look, sweetheart, I already went through an

emergency without a contact number. I think you'll do okay without it now." He glared at her and this time she took a step backward, her pen still hovering over the clipboard she was carrying.

"The police need to talk to you about pressing charges." She bit her lip, running her finger nervously along one side of the clipboard.

"I'm not pressing charges. I don't care about the bike. It can be replaced. If they say they want to talk to me, tell them that I'm in a coma, okay?" He stopped, as a fresh wave of pain washed over him.

"But sir, that would be lying."

Simon took a breath, his anger too easily coming to the surface. "Just go," he snapped. He closed his eyes. For four days he had been in constant pain. Each time he thought it was getting better, the physiotherapist came and got him moving around and the agony would start all over again.

He felt the fuzziness of the painkiller slowly overtaking him and he fought it even as he welcomed it. Out of control, he thought, I hate being out of control. He drifted along for timeless moments. Then…

"Hello, Simon. How are you doing?"

That voice, he thought, forcing his eyes open.

Caitlin stood beside the bed, a stethoscope clipped around her neck. Her hair was pulled back away from her face enhancing the delicate line of her chin, her narrow nose, eyebrows that winged upward from soft green eyes. He wished he didn't hurt so much. He wished he had the strength to reach up, pull her close to him and kiss that gently curving mouth.

But all he could do was lie immobile with metal and screws holding his leg together and some kind of wrap covering it. A cripple. It wasn't fair, he thought.

She unrolled a blood pressure cuff and gently raised his good arm, slipping it around. Her hands were cool, her touch careful.

"Hi yourself, angel," he said slowly. "You working now?"

"Yes. I'll be taking care of you for the next twelve hours." She pressurized the cuff and she slipped the stethoscope in her ears.

"Sounds like a wonderful twelve hours."

She only set the stethoscope on his arm and listened. When she was done she pulled the cuff off, rolled it up and tucked it behind the fixture on the wall. She was all aloof efficiency and order and it bugged Simon more than he liked to admit.

When her soft hands lifted his wrist to take his pulse, he held his breath, knowing that the other nurses counted his respirations while they thought he wasn't looking. She dropped his wrist and pulled the stethoscope out of her ears.

Didn't even notice, he thought feeling childishly disappointed.

She pulled a pen and pad out of her pocket and

made a few quick notes. "Let's see, blood pressure normal, pulse strong, respirations—" Caitlin stopped and glanced sidelong at Simon "—normal, now."

He grinned back at her. "I guess you know all the tricks," he said.

"I'd say you need to get out more when someone your age needs to resort to tricks to get extra attention," she said, her voice dry.

"I got yours, didn't I?"

Caitlin looked up at him. "What you *got* was a nurse doing her job."

"And being so aloof is also part of your job?" Simon groused. He didn't like hearing that professional tone of voice. Not from a woman who looked like an angel with her wings clipped. "You weren't like that before."

"I wasn't working before," she said briskly. She picked up the machine that took his temperature and clipped a new earpiece on. "Turn your head to the side, please."

"Whatever happened to good old thermometers?" he asked as she inserted it in his ear.

It beeped and she took it out. "Good old thermometers aren't as quick or reliable." She marked something down and slipped the notepad in her pocket. "Of course, it was a great way to keep the patient quiet," she said with a quick lift of her eyebrows at him.

He smiled at that. She returned it with one of her own that made Simon catch his breath.

"How have you been feeling?" she said, her voice lowering, taking on a softer tone.

She had switched from efficient nurse to the caring woman who had stayed with him a whole night. He couldn't stop his response to her warmth and concern. "It's bad," he said simply.

"I know," she said softly. "But you fight the pain and the medication stops you from doing that. You may feel out of it, but you need to let your body rest so you can heal."

"I can't get out of here soon enough."

Caitlin shook her head. "I wouldn't rush it. You won't be walking when you do and you'll need therapy and home care. You'll probably be walking with the help of a walker, then crutches, then a cane. A broken femur is a huge injury and takes a long time to heal."

Simon nodded, not wanting to hear what she had to say or the vulnerability it represented.

"Where is home?" she asked suddenly.

"I've just got an apartment along the bay in Vancouver, on the mainland." Hardly home. More like a home base.

"You're going to need some help the first couple of weeks. Is there anyone who can come or will you have to hire a nurse?" She looked down at him, her one eyebrow lifted questioningly, but Simon didn't want to bite. She didn't need to know there was no one he could ask. He didn't want to be reminded of his lack of family—reminded that he had lost touch with anyone who had ever meant anything to him. It made his life less complicated. He had never needed anyone. Oscar's words came back to haunt him. They were frighteningly appropriate.

She waited a moment, then with a gentle sigh, turned his IV stand around and read some figures off it. He knew that once she was done recording all the numbers that nurses seemed so awfully fond of, she would be gone until later on this evening when she would check his dressings. Perversely he didn't want her to go.

"Why do I need help?" he asked, reluctantly acknowledging her previous comment.

"Because you're not going to be able to move around very easily. You'll need help with bathing and moving around. You'll still be in pain...."

"I'll figure something out."

Caitlin looked down at him. "What about your work?"

"I work for myself. Have for years."

"Is that why you are so tough and independent?"

Simon heard the slight note of censure in her voice and bristled. "I've had to learn from early on to take care of myself, find my own way."

"Well, for now you're in our capable hands."

"And are you going to hold me in those capable hands?" he asked with a wink.

"See you later, Mr. Steele." And with that she turned and left.

Chapter Five

Caitlin pushed her chair back from the computer and stretched. She had trouble falling asleep yesterday after working her first night shift. It always happened. So she was feeling a little woozy. All the patients were asleep.

Except one. Simon.

She had to check his dressings. Now was as good a time as any. She had put it off for a while, hoping one of the other nurses on the team would, but they all seemed to avoid him.

Caitlin had avoided him, too. She was uncomfortable around him.

She walked into the room. The patient just recently admitted was asleep. His name was Shane. Football injury. Same temperament as Simon, just a little younger.

"Hey, company. Sit down, talk to me," Simon said

as she walked around the curtain dividing him and Shane.

"Sorry. Can't oblige." She checked his IV while she spoke, adjusting the flow. She turned back to him and lifted his bedsheet, folding it back to check his incision. Caitlin frowned as she rolled back the wrap that held the dressings in place. She bent over to take a closer look at the incision. It was redder than it should be.

"Does this hurt?"

"C'mon, Caitlin, it always hurts." He reached up and laid a warm hand on her arm, his finger moving up and down her arm in a caressing motion.

She felt her heart flutter at his touch and glanced sidelong at him. His eyes were crinkled up at the corners, and she didn't like the way he was smiling at her. It looked polished, purposeful, fake.

She took his hand and laid it back on the bed, angry at her own reaction. Simon was an accomplished flirt. She would do well to remember that.

"Does it hurt more than usual?" she asked, touching the skin lightly, forcing her mind back to her job. She frowned. His skin felt unusually warm.

"I don't know," he said. "Like I said, it always hurts." He placed his hand on his chest and sighed. "Just like my heart."

"Give it a rest, Mr. Steele," she said, now truly ticked with him. He was bored and she was overreacting.

She frowned and lowered the sheet, then walked around the bed to his other side. "Let me see your arm, please."

"My goodness, aren't you all efficiency tonight?" he said, his voice suddenly testy.

Caitlin glanced at him, then away. He had been alternately flirtatious and cranky ever since she had come on duty this evening. Guys usually were ornery after a few days of being confined to bed, but Simon had been getting worse each hour she worked. It didn't help that his sleep had been interrupted when they brought the new admission into his room. Things were always busy the first hour after a patient came up from surgery, and Simon had been irritable at the constant comings and goings.

She carefully peeled back the tape, unable to avoid pulling the hairs sprinkled over his forearm.

He sucked in his breath at the pain. "That hurts, angel."

"Sorry," she murmured automatically, quickly pulling back the rest of the dressing.

He took a deep breath and then another, slowly relaxing. "That apology didn't sound too sincere, Caitlin," he said quietly.

"Probably not," she said evenly, determined not to let him get under her skin.

Simon laughed at that. Their eyes met and held, and Caitlin again felt her heart give a little kick. And again, she berated herself for her reaction. He was demanding and confusing, turning his charm on and off at will, yet she couldn't seem to reason her way past her reaction to him.

Because each time she saw him, what she remembered most was the feel of his hand clutching hers, the entreaty in his eyes, his vulnerability.

She looked down at what she was doing, forcing her mind back to the task at hand. She frowned. "Is your arm feeling itchy yet?"

"Do I have that to look forward to as well?"

Caitlin shrugged. "If it's itchy, that's a sign that it's healing."

"Well, it's not."

"I'll change this for now."

"Why are you frowning?" Simon caught her hand in his, tugging on it.

"I'm a little concerned about infection," she said, pulling on her hand. But Simon was a lot stronger now than he was at first, and he wouldn't let go.

"You're a good nurse, Caitlin," he said with a wry grin.

"It's my job. Now let go of my hand so I can do it."

"Nurse means 'to take care of,'" he said, his voice lowering. He ran his thumb over the knuckles of her hand, his eyes on hers. "I want you to stay and talk to me, take care of me."

Caitlin wanted to be angry with him, wanted to

dislike what he was doing. She wanted to pull away, but his hand was warm, his gaze compelling.

"Just talk," he said softly, tugging on her hand. "I'm lonely."

Caitlin forced herself to look away, reluctantly pulling her hand free. What was wrong with her? She knew virtually nothing about this man and here she was, at his bedside, holding on to his hand. Again.

"I've got to get some clean dressings," she said, turning away. "I'll be right back."

"I'll be waiting."

Caitlin grimaced at how that sounded. "I didn't mean it like that," she muttered to herself as she marched to the supply room. Once there she stopped a moment, frustrated. She, a professional nurse who prided herself on her objectivity, had let a patient get to her.

She shook her head as if to dispel the feelings she had experienced in the room a few moments ago. She straightened her shoulders, and wheeled the dressing cart back to his room.

He lay looking out the darkened window to the night outside. Most patients liked to have the curtains shut during the evening, but Simon always had his open. The light above his bed illuminated his reflection in the large sheet of glass.

But as Caitlin paused at the foot of his bed, she seemed to sense that he was looking beyond his reflection in the window, beyond the lights of Nanaimo that spread out below him. He seemed to be in another place and for a moment, she wanted to know where.

She sighed, exasperated with herself. Wasn't it just twenty seconds ago that she prayed for detachment?

She walked between him and the window, pushing the cart to the side of his bed.

Caitlin usually liked to explain what she was doing to patients, just in case they had any concerns. This time, however, she worked in silence, careful not to hurt Simon any more than she had to.

When she was done, she tidied up and turned to leave.

"Do you have family, Caitlin?" Simon asked suddenly.

Caitlin paused, curious as to why he would ask. "Yes. I have two sisters and one brother."

"Do they live around here?"

"No. My brother lives in Toronto, my older sister in Portland, Oregon, and my younger sister and her husband live in Vancouver."

"They're all married and you're not?"

It was more of a statement than a question, but it still sounded mocking to her. And it sounded exactly like her mother.

"That happens sometimes," she said dryly.

Fortunately even he sensed that he had gone too far.

"What about parents?"

Caitlin smiled, wondering if he was joking. "Parents usually come with the package."

"No, they don't." His voice was quiet and when Simon turned to look at her, his eyes were devoid of expression.

"I remember you said something about a foster home the first time I talked to you. Were you there all your life?"

Simon laughed shortly, then turned his head again, not answering her question. Caitlin waited a moment wondering if he would say anything more. When he didn't, she left, puzzled as to why he had even asked her the questions.

You're a fool, Simon Steele, or whoever you are. Don't get to know her, don't ask her questions. She's just a nurse, not an angel. When she stopped to help you she was just doing what she was trained to.

Including staying the whole night with you?

Simon closed his eyes, willing away the picture of Caitlin, her mouth relaxed, her hair spread out on her arms that night she slept at the foot of the hospital bed. So beautiful, so peaceful. He didn't want to wonder why she had stayed the night, why she wasn't married. He had almost asked her if she had a boyfriend. As if that should matter to him.

Forget her, Simon, he reminded himself, she's not your type.

Of course, he didn't know anymore what his type was. He used to be attracted to more obvious women—the ones who knew how to play the game. The ones he could date a few times then forget to call. The ones who didn't require commitment. The ones who didn't get close.

But the past few years he'd grown weary of the games, the empty talk. He was tired of the emptiness of the relationships in his life.

When the nurses asked about next of kin, he almost mentioned his older brother Jake. Then he stopped himself. The last time he'd spoken with Jake was from a pay phone. Simon had run away from his last foster home and wanted Jake to join him in his search for their biological mother. Jake had refused. When Simon had told him that he had to choose between Jake's current foster parents or him, Jake had chosen the Prins family.

Simon told Jake that he'd never hear from him again. He didn't need Jake. He didn't need anybody. He would make it on his own.

And he had.

His fortunes went up and down, but he never cared. It was a game and one he was good at because it only required luck, some intuition and a lot of nerve.

And he'd done well. But as his bank account grew, his own dissatisfaction increased proportionately. He had indulged in the toys—a few fancy cars, a sailboat, his motorbike. He lived out of hotels, indulging and pampering himself. He bought what he wanted when he wanted, but as soon as he owned what he wanted he lost interest.

So he'd finally bought a condo in Vancouver, hoping that establishing some kind of home base would give him whatever it was that eluded him. Happiness, contentment. He wasn't sure. He only knew that the old restlessness that sent him out on the road as a young man had captured him again. He had promised himself once he'd settled down, once he'd made it, he'd contact Jake. But as each year passed it got harder. His pride kept him back. And his shame. For he knew that his life was still not what it should be and he didn't need to be reminded.

Now he lay in a hospital bed in a city that was supposed to be only a quick side trip, wishing he could get on with his life.

Tired of his own thoughts, he blew out his breath and pushed the Call button again. He didn't care if Caitlin got angry with him, he was hurting and bored. Not a good combination.

She came after a few minutes, appearing at his bedside to turn off his pager. She turned to him, her arms crossed over her stomach. "What can I do for you?"

Simon had to give her a lot of credit. He knew she was ticked but you couldn't tell from her voice. He didn't know exactly how he knew. He just did.

"That's not really a nurse's uniform is it?" he asked taking another look at her aqua pantsuit topped with a sweater in a paler shade.

"I'm sure you didn't summon me to discuss fashion," she said quietly. She glanced at his IV and walked to the foot of his bed. "Do you want me to lower the bed for you. You really should be sleeping."

"I'm tired of sleeping, of being drugged and lying here."

"Good. That means you're getting better." She flashed him a quick smile and bent over to crank the head of his bed down anyhow.

"Don't. Please." He didn't know where the "please" came from. It wasn't like him to beg.

She straightened. "You really need to sleep, Simon."

Her voice was no-nonsense and firm but hearing her say his name gave him a jolt. "I can't. I'm bored, and everything still hurts. I feel like a child."

"Do you want something to read?"

"I've read all the magazines already."

"What about books?"

Simon looked away, frowning, trying to remember the last book he read. "Maybe," he said with a shrug.

"We've got some Westerns, which might appeal to a modern-day cowboy like you, some science fiction, mysteries, thrillers—the usual cross section."

"I don't like fiction. Why don't you just sit and talk to me?"

Caitlin shook her head and walked over to the side of his bed, leaning against the metal radiator that ran along the wall below the window. "You are probably my most persistent patient. It's one o'clock in the morning, you really need to sleep."

"So you said." He smiled at her and folded his hands on his chest. She looked like she was willing to stay awhile, which suited him just fine. "How long have you been working here?"

"Five years."

He raised his eyebrows at that. "That long?"

"What do you mean?"

"I don't think I held a job down longer than a year."

"What did you do?"

Simon hesitated, lifting his thumbs and inspecting them. "This and that."

"Sounds fishy," Caitlin said, dropping her head to one side, as if inspecting him.

"Not really." He frowned at her. "Did you grow up here?"

She nodded, her head still angled slightly sideways. "My parents own a house close to the ferry terminal. I've lived there all my life."

"Tire swing, tree house, big porch?"

"Yes, actually." She smiled and once again Simon felt a peculiar tightness in his chest and once again he wondered why she had this effect on him. "My dad built us a tree house and Mom helped us furnish it."

"Us being the brother and sisters?" He couldn't help the sardonic tone in his voice. "Sounds very cozy and small-town America."

Caitlin shrugged. "It was, until I pushed Tony off the ladder because he and his friends were chasing me. He ended up with a broken leg, and I ended up being banished from the tree house for a month."

"But you nursed him back to health, and that's how you discovered you wanted to be a nurse?"

"Right," Caitlin said with a short laugh. "Tony wouldn't let me within five feet of him, then or now. We weren't close then. Unfortunately we still aren't."

Simon heard the plaintive note in her voice and couldn't stop himself from asking, "Why not?"

"My brother has made some pretty poor choices in his life that we've had a hard time living with."

"That sounds 'Caitlinese' for he messed up."

Caitlin tilted her shoulder up in a light shrug. "I guess that was full of euphemisms." She held his gaze as if weighing his reaction. "Tony got involved with a gang when he was young. They ran wild, and he ran with them. He married one of the girls, moved to Toronto and we haven't heard from him since."

"The black sheep of the cozy family."

"Why do you say that with such sarcasm?"

Simon didn't reply, not sure himself. He had spent

most of his life disdaining family, so it just came naturally. No one had challenged him on that before.

"Our family is close, but we're not an unusual group of people," Caitlin continued, pushing herself away from the radiator. "Stable American families are more common than television, newspapers and movies would have us believe."

"And you probably pray before every meal, too."

Caitlin drew in a slow breath, as if weighing her answer. "As a matter of fact we do. We read the Bible regularly, and we struggle each day to live out our faith in all the things we do and say. Tony gets mentioned in just about every prayer that gets uttered either aloud or in quiet."

Caitlin spoke quietly, but Simon easily heard the sincerity in her words. They intruded upon a part of his life he thought he had safely pushed aside. He tried to hold her steady gaze, to keep his eyes on her soft green ones, reaching for the sarcasm he knew would push her away from the place she had ventured too close to.

"Nice to know I'm in such good company."

"What do you mean?"

He winked at her, but it lacked conviction on his part. "You prayed for me, too," he said sarcastically. "Do you still pray for me?"

She held his eyes captive, her expression serious. "Yes I do, Simon." Her voice was quiet, her words simple, yet what she said shook him to the core. "Do you need anything else?"

He watched her a moment, noting the change in her expression at his tone and suddenly disliking it more than he thought he would, but knowing he had to take this through to the end. "I still need something to read."

She reached behind her and pulled open the drawer of his bedside table. She pulled out a Bible and laid it gently beside his hand. "You said you didn't like reading fiction, this might be just the thing."

And with that she left.

Chapter Six

"Cup of tea, honey?"

"That sounds wonderful." Caitlin yawned, shooed the cat off the wooden chair and sat down at the kitchen table. She finger-combed her hair, still damp from her shower as she looked around the brightly lit room, smiling.

Watching her mother move unhurriedly around the kitchen gave her a sense of order and continuity. As long as she could remember, her mother made her tea when she woke up whether it was in the morning for a regular day of school or work or in midafternoon when she started working shifts.

Her mother set a steaming mug in front of her. Caitlin wrapped her hands around it, stifling another yawn.

"And how was work?" her mother asked, sitting down at the table close to Caitlin, holding her own cup.

"Busy." She spooned sugar into her tea. "Where's Rachel?"

"She and Jonathon packed a picnic and headed up to Denman Island. They were hoping to check out the market there." Her mother took a careful sip of tea and brushed a lock of graying hair out of her face. "You could have gone with them if you hadn't decided to work."

Caitlin shrugged, ignoring her mother's heavy hint and the guilt that came with it. Spending time with her sister should be more important than working but it wasn't.

Her mother had tried to convince her she needed time at home to catch her breath. She didn't understand Caitlin's desire to get busy, to work in an effort to push aside what had happened, to get on with her life.

"I got a phone call last night." Her mother's soft voice broke the silence.

"From…" Caitlin prompted, her heart fluttering at the intensity of her mother's gaze.

"Charles."

I knew she was going to say that, Caitlin thought. "What did he want?" she asked, putting down her cup.

"He said he still had your suitcase and was hoping to drop it off."

Caitlin had forgotten about the arrangements she and Charles had made for their holiday. A day before their fateful date she had brought her clothes to his parents' place. They were to bring it to the cabin so that Caitlin and Charles could leave directly for Pender Island after supper.

"What did you tell him?"

Jean Severn pulled in her lips, looking down at her cup of tea. "I told him when you would be awake, but he said he would bring it to the hospital once he was done work."

"Why didn't you tell him to just bring it here?" Caitlin didn't want to see him again.

Jean looked up with an encouraging smile. "I thought he might want to talk to you. Maybe he wants to get back together...."

"Don't even say it, mother," Caitlin said, raising her hand in warning. "He's moving to L.A. He doesn't want to commit himself. We've been through this before."

Caitlin knew her mother had loved Charles and had such high hopes for the two of them. That those hopes had been dashed was more of a disappointment to her than it had been to Caitlin.

"How many evening shifts are you going to be working?" her mother asked, wisely changing the subject.

"I've already done three, so I'll be working two more."

"Too bad your tickets to Portland are booked already, otherwise you could leave earlier."

Caitlin shrugged. "Doesn't matter. Maybe I'll head up-island myself. Hit Hornby Island for a while, go up to Miracle Beach."

"You don't sound very enthusiastic about that," her mother said intuitively.

"You're right. I'm just thinking aloud." Caitlin pulled one leg up on the chair hugging it. "I'm just feeling a little mixed up right now. Maybe I kept dating Charles because I thought if I let him go, who else would I have?" Caitlin rubbed her chin on her worn jeans, feeling distinctly melancholy. "I think we were just a convenience to each other."

"You and Charles were never a passionate couple, Caity, but you were never a passionate person. You've always liked things orderly and neat. I never had to nag you to clean up your room like I did your siblings."

"You make me sound boring."

Jean leaned over and ran her hand over Caitlin's cheek. "You are anything but boring, Caitlin. You have a caring, steady nature and a solid faith I know many people envy."

I still sound boring, Caitlin thought. Nice, but boring. But she smiled at her mother, secure in the love that surrounded her. "And you're a good mom." She leaned her head against her mother's shoulder. "I feel like I'm still in high school, coming home and dumping on you."

Jean stroked Caitlin's hair, rubbing her chin over Caitlin's head. "I am glad you can. I pray you will find some direction in your life. I know that God isn't..."

"...through with me yet," Caitlin interrupted, finishing the familiar saying with a smile. She straightened and gave her mother a quick kiss. "Let's see, what else could you tell me. I'm still young and there's lots of other fish in the sea. There's not a pot so crooked that a lid doesn't fit on it." There were many more homilies her mother often used and all had to do with finding someone in her life. Marriage, the ultimate goal.

Jean shook her head and tousled her daughter's hair. "That's enough, you pest. You had better head upstairs and get dressed if you want to get to work on time."

Caitlin stood up, looking down on her mother. Much as she teased her mother about her truisms, she also knew that there was a lot of truth in those simple phrases. Truth and love dispensed in equal measure.

She smiled, and bending over, dropped a kiss on her mother's forehead. "I love you, Mom. I hope you know that."

"Yes, I do." Jean Severn smiled up at her daughter. "You're a wonderful daughter and a wonderful person. That hasn't changed."

* * *

"And how have our model patients been doing?" Caitlin walked into the hospital room and stopped by Shane's table. Schoolbooks, papers and cards covered it. He was hunched over a handheld computer game, ignoring her.

"Hey, you little twerp," Simon said from the bed beside him, "Caitlin asked you a question."

Shane looked up at that, his eyes opening wide when he saw Caitlin. He laid down the game, the frown on his face fading away to be replaced by a sheepish grin. "Sorry," he said, pushing himself to a sitting position. "I didn't know it was you." He looked up at her again, smiling.

"That's okay," Caitlin said, puzzled at the change.

Yesterday he had been snappy. Now he seemed eager to please.

"You working tonight?" he asked pulling the table closer. He laughed shortly. "Of course you are," he said without giving her a chance to reply. "That's why you're here. Sorry."

Caitlin could see he was embarrassed and resisted the urge to smile. "I'm just checking up on everyone. Usual beginning-of-the-shift stuff."

"Well, thanks."

"I noticed you had a bunch of visitors today."

Shane nodded, relaxing enough to sit back. "Friends from school, some of the teammates."

"The day nurse told me your girlfriend came," Caitlin prompted, smiling now.

"Well, she's just a friend. We're sort of seeing each other, but not really."

"I wish my girlfriends treated me like that," Simon interjected from his side of the room. Caitlin turned to him with a frown, and he only winked at her. "She was hanging on him like a bad suit."

Shane looked down at his computer game. "Well, she'll dump me quick enough, when she finds out I can't play football anymore," he muttered.

"Oh, she'll stick around for a while," Simon disagreed, his voice holding that world-weary tone that set Caitlin's teeth on edge. "As long as you've got money, you'll be okay."

"Thanks for your input, Simon." Caitlin's voice took on a fake sweetness as she turned to him. "I'll talk to you later." And with that she pulled the curtain between them. It was a flimsy barrier, he could still hear everything she said to Shane, but it gave the idea of privacy. Hopefully Simon would take the hint.

"Do you think she went out with you just because you are a football player?" Caitlin asked, lowering her voice.

"Maybe." Shane lifted one shoulder in a negligent shrug. "But that doesn't matter anymore." He looked up and tried out a smile that aimed for the same casual familiarity that Simon had mastered to perfection. But Shane's missed the mark. Obviously not as experienced, Caitlin thought.

"I'm sure the fact that you won't play football doesn't matter as much to her as it does to you," she said, her voice taking on a brisk, reassuring tone. "And who knows. Once you get mobile, you might be surprised what you can do yet." She left, fighting the urge to smile.

"You're looking mighty cheerful," Simon said as she came around the curtain.

Caitlin shook her head as she glanced at him. "And you seem pretty good compared to what your chart says. Your temperature is up a bit, and you look flushed."

"I'm fine." Simon winked at her then tried to push himself up with his hands. He sucked in a quick breath through clenched teeth, his eyes shut. He lay still for a moment then was about to try again.

"Don't, Simon." Caitlin laid a warning hand on his shoulder. "Here, I'll put another pillow behind your back, then you don't have to move."

He nodded weakly, showing to Caitlin how deep his agony really was. She got a pillow from the foot of his bed and carefully inserted it behind him. He was breathing with slow, controlled breaths, riding out the pain. He lay back against the pillow which allowed him to sit up a little higher. "Thanks, angel," he said, pulling in another slow, deep breath, as he smiled up at her.

Her heart softened as their eyes met. While she had thankfully never had to endure what many of her patients had, experience had given her an idea of how they felt. Seeing a man of Simon's age and strength made so weak and helpless always wounded her deeply.

He slowly settled back, relaxing now. "Are you going to stick around awhile? My girlfriend didn't come today."

Caitlin felt a slight jolt of disappointment. So, he had a girlfriend after all. "Does she know you're here?" she asked, trying to sound nonchalant.

Simon angled a grin up at her. "She doesn't even know I exist. I don't have a girlfriend."

"Oh. I see." Caitlin didn't see, though. She didn't see why that should matter to her. She didn't see why she should care. But she did.

"But Shane over there does have a girlfriend, even though he doesn't want you to think so." He waggled a finger. "Come here," he whispered. "I've got to tell you something."

Puzzled, she stepped closer to the bed, bending down slightly.

"You're too far away," he whispered.

Caitlin bent nearer, disconcerted to feel Simon's hand on her neck, pulling her down.

"I think that boy likes you."

Caitlin heard his words, but even more than that, she felt his warm breath feather her hair, felt her own breath slow at his touch. She pulled abruptly away, her heart pushing against her chest. "Don't be absurd," she said, quickly trying to cover up her reaction to him. What was wrong with her?

"I'm not absurd." Simon smiled up at her, his mouth curved in a mischievous smile that showed her quite clearly what kind of a man he really was. "And you know what? I have a crush on you, too." He cocked his head, raising his eyebrows suggestively and Caitlin turned away, disgusted with him and even more, herself. In spite of what she knew about him, his smile still gave her a slight jolt.

"I'll check on you later," was all she said.

She made the rest of her rounds. The next two patients she saw were a good balance to Simon and his innuendoes and leading comments. He was a study in frustration. It seemed each time he showed his vulnerability, he had to counteract that with some ridiculous behavior.

Caitlin continued her rounds, checking her patients' vitals. When she stopped to check on Shane again, his parents had him laughing so she left him alone for now. The curtain was drawn between his and Simon's beds and when she stopped on Simon's side, it was to find him with the head of his bed elevated as he stared at the curtain dividing the room. He seemed to be listening to the chatter going on beside him. If Caitlin didn't know him better, she would say his expression was almost wistful.

Her earlier pique with him had dissipated in the routine of her work. Once again she found herself watching him, wondering who he really was and where he really came from, why no one visited him or phoned. Not even the elusive Oscar.

He turned his head and caught her looking. He gave her a bold wink and sly grin which completely broke the very temporary mood.

"You still love me, angel?"

I give up on this man, Caitlin thought. She walked to his side, clipping the stethoscope in her ears. "How are you feeling?" she asked as she put on the blood pressure cuff.

He held her gaze a moment, then looked away. "Not great," he said succinctly.

His face was still flushed, and she laid her hand on his forehead. It was warm.

"Have you been feeling shaky, or trembly at all?"

"Not really." He picked up the book he had been reading and closed it. "Can you put this back on the table?"

Caitlin took the book, surprised to see that it was the Bible. She glanced at Simon, but he was looking sidelong at the curtain again, listening to the voices beyond so she laid it beside the bed.

He laid his head back and sighed, his eyes squeezed shut. Caitlin was concerned. By now she knew Simon well enough to realize he wouldn't tell her if he was dying.

She took his temperature.

"Still good. Only .04 above normal. Must be something else," she murmured, making a note on his chart.

"How often do you hear from your brother in Toronto?" Simon asked. "The black sheep."

Caitlin felt taken aback, surprised that he remembered, wondering why he brought it up. "My parents haven't heard from him in four years. We don't know where he lives anymore."

"And what would you do if he showed up on your doorstep?" Simon opened his eyes, holding hers with a steady gaze.

"Let him in. Feed him and then give him a smack for making us worry about him."

"Would you forgive him for making you worry?"

"Of course."

Simon quirked an eyebrow up at her, his expression slightly cynical. "You say that so easily. C'mon," he urged. "Try to imagine him coming back, then tell me you'd just let him in."

Caitlin looked past Simon, lost herself for a moment in memories and wishes. "You're right. I said that quite easily. I think it would be hard. But in spite of never being close, he's still my brother." Caitlin looked back at Simon. "That will never change no matter how I wish it. My mother and father love him dearly. For their sake as much as my own I would probably forgive him. I believe God has forgiven me a whole lot more."

"Sort of like the parable of the debtors."

"Which one do you mean?"

"You know. The one where the king forgave a man a huge debt and then the man turns around and sends one of his debtors to prison for an even smaller debt."

"That would be the one," she said, surprised that he knew it. "How did you know that?"

"My adoptive father used to read the Bible to us pretty regularly." Simon shrugged as if uncomfortable admitting even that much.

"I'm glad to hear that." She smiled, pleased to find out that he had some faith training in his life. It made him more approachable somehow. "I'll be back in half an hour, and I'll check your temperature again. I'm a little concerned about how you're feeling."

She looked down at him, still holding the thermometer. His hazel eyes held hers and she couldn't look away. She felt as if she were drifting toward him, falling, losing herself in his mesmerizing gaze.

"Caitlin." His voice was quiet, barely above a whisper and the sound of it speaking her name created a subtle intimacy.

She couldn't look away, didn't want to.

She was standing close to him, and when he reached up to touch her, to gently run his fingers along her elbow, she couldn't stop him.

"What are you doing to me?" he murmured,

stroking her upper arm with light movements of his fingers, his eyes warm, soft, holding hers. "You save my life, you stay with me, you take care of me, you've even got me reading the Bible, something I haven't done in years." He laughed lightly, his fingers encircling her arm with a warmth that quickened her pulse. He gave her a light shake, as if in reprimand. "What are you really, Caitlin? An angel?"

Caitlin swallowed, trying to find her breath. "I'm just a nurse," she replied, her own voice tense with suppressed emotion.

The words, spoken aloud, were a palpable reminder of where she was and who she was. "Just a nurse," she repeated again. Shaken, she pulled away and without looking back, left.

She managed to make it to the desk, sat down behind its high wall and dropped her face into her hands. What was happening to her? She who prided herself on her professionalism, her detachment, her ability to calmly assess a situation was getting drawn into something that was moving out of her control.

She was falling for a patient.

All through her training warnings against precisely that had been drilled into each nurse. The dangers of the enforced intimacy of the patient-nurse relationship. The helplessness of a patient creating a false romanticism. Bored patients who whiled away their time trying to get nurses to pay attention to them.

Simon was all the warnings she had ever heard, all the warnings she had ever given other student nurses, wrapped up in one dangerous package. And she was falling for him.

Blowing out a sigh, she pulled her hands over her face, resting her fingers against her mouth. She had been crazy to come back to work so soon after breaking up with Charles. She thought it would help. But she was emotionally vulnerable and Simon was bored and carelessly handsome.

A bad combination all the way around.

Chapter Seven

Simon closed his eyes, wishing sleep would drift over his mind, pulling with it the thoughts that wouldn't stop. But sleep was the one thing he couldn't accomplish through force of will.

At the bed beside him, Shane's parents were saying goodbye. The quiet sound of their voices created an unexpected sorrow he disliked.

All evening people had come and gone through this room, and the only people who stopped by his bed were Caitlin and the cleaning lady. He wasn't a maudlin sort. Ever since he and his brother Jake had been split up he knew that to need people was to give them an edge over you. And once they had an edge over you, they were in charge.

The solution was easy. Keep relationships light and superficial and don't let anyone get close. He had accomplished both quite well.

But that meant Simon now lay, alone, in a hospital bed and no one knew or cared.

Snap out of it Simon, he reprimanded himself. You want it this way. You don't want anyone intruding on your life with their expectations, telling you what to do.

He heard the scrape of chairs beside him, heard Shane's mother murmur, "Make sure you get enough rest, honey."

"Don't go racing down the hall," his sister added with an attempt at humor.

"Like I could," Shane replied but his voice didn't have the petulant whine of a few days ago.

"We'll come by again tomorrow," Shane's father said. Simon didn't want to look, but did anyhow. He saw the faint shadow of someone bending over the head of the bed, then another and another.

"Love you, Shane," the mother whispered.

"Love you too, Mom," he whispered back.

Simon turned his head back to the window. Wasn't that cute, he thought. Mom and Dad and sister kissing Shane goodbye. He didn't think anyone did that anymore. He didn't think anyone did that, ever.

He closed his eyes, but he couldn't erase the image. He wondered what it would have been like, at Shane's age, to have lived with adults who touched in kindness instead of in anger. Parents who cared, who loved, who surrounded you in times of need.

Once in his life he had been surrounded with love. The love of his adoptive father, Tom Steele. Once he had been tucked in and kissed goodnight by his adoptive father. But that was in another age, another life.

"Do you want me to turn off your light?"

Caitlin's soft voice gave him a start. He opened his eyes, to see her standing beside his bed.

"No," he replied, unable to keep his eyes off her. "I can't sleep."

"You have to. You haven't been able to sleep for a couple of nights now." Caitlin frowned, looking concerned as she stepped closer. She fussed with his sheet, folded his blanket back—little maternal things that touched on a hidden sorrow, reinforcing the mood brought on by Shane's family.

Her hair was loose this evening, framing her delicate features. Her eyes looked brighter, her cheeks pinker and her lips shone.

"You really are beautiful," he couldn't help but say.

Caitlin's cheeks grew even pinker. She was blushing, he thought with a measure of wonder. Without thinking, he reached out and took her hand.

Maybe it was the loneliness, maybe it was the sappy mood he had worked himself into, but when he felt her delicate fingers in his, he couldn't stop himself. He lifted her hand to his face and pressed a kiss in her palm.

And what was even more amazing, she let him. He felt her fingers curve around his cheek, brushing it lightly, then she slowly pulled her hand back.

"How are you feeling?" she asked, sounding breathless.

Like I should be standing up, with my arms around you, kissing you, he thought, sucking in a deep breath. "I'll be okay," was all he could say. He really had to get out of here. This woman was starting to get to him.

Caitlin laid the back of her hand on his forehead and frowned. "You're not feverish, thank the Lord."

"Why thank him?' he said, trying for his usual flippant attitude, the one he knew she hated. Anything to avert his reaction to her gentle touch. "He didn't have anything to do with this."

Caitlin only smiled. "I think He did."

"You been praying again?"

"Yes."

"I told you not to do that." Her talk of prayer always made him uncomfortable. Just like reading the Bible had. It reminded him of living with Tom Steele and Jake.

"Well, I did it anyhow."

"Like I said before, you're wasting your time. I'm just a blip in your life, sweet Caitlin." Simon could tell from the look on her face he had hurt her, which was what he intended to do.

Then why did it bother him, he wondered. "So what do you want from me now?"

She was supposed to say "Nothing" and then leave. She was supposed to stop tormenting him with her sincerity, her concern, her talk of prayers. Instead she pulled a chair close and sat down beside him in spite of how he had just talked to her.

"Simon, isn't there anyone we can call, anyone who we should tell about your accident?"

"There's no one else."

"You had said something about a foster home…."

"I've been in a bunch of them, Caitlin." Simon turned to face her, unable to keep the bitterness out of his voice. "I ran away from just about every one of them. They don't care. The very nature of foster homes is temporary."

"Why did you run away?"

Simon held her soft gaze, a gentle pain building in his chest and warnings ringing in his head. But he was lonely and in pain, and Caitlin was here. She'd be out of his life in a week anyhow so he took a chance and told her the truth. "Because it was easier than letting someone get close," he said finally. "At least that's what the counselors always said."

"You've been to counseling?"

"Seeing a counselor doesn't make me crazy you know."

"Don't be so defensive," she chided, lightly shaking her head. "Seeing a counselor is a sign of strength, not weakness."

Simon felt himself relax at what she said, felt

that peculiar tension that always gripped him when she was around, loosen. "I saw some when I was in foster care, and I went a bunch of times in the past few years."

"So how old were you when you ended up on your own?"

"Sixteen."

"Wouldn't you have been in care until you were eighteen?"

Simon shrugged. "If I had followed the rules, yes. But I took off from the treatment foster home they put me."

"Where did you go from there?"

"I ended up hitching a ride with a bunch of tree planters. They told me about the good money they made and I joined them."

"And then…" she prompted, smiling in encouragement.

"Then I moved from one job to another. I made good money tree planting, worked on the rigs offshore, saved my money and invested it."

"So what do you do now?"

"This and that. I play the stock market, own some property. Oscar takes care of the details." He caught her gaze and smiled. "I've done well for myself. I've got a lot of money. I can do pretty much what I please." Simon stopped himself. He sounded as if he were trying to impress her and maybe in a way he was. He had gotten where he was by virtue of his own hard work, his own luck and making his own choices. "I've been luckier in the second part of my life than the first."

"Until now," she said, her mouth curving up.

He swallowed, her smile winding around his heart, warming and softening it as he held her eyes with his own. She didn't look away and slowly all else drifted away, meaningless, unknown. His past, his need for independence all seemed to disappear. There was only him and Caitlin. It seemed too right to reach out, to feather his fingers against her soft cheek. She turned her face oh-so-slightly, her eyes drifting shut as her hand came up to hold his hand close to her face.

They stayed thus, the tenuous connection holding them, creating a fragile bond. Then a cart rattled past the door and Caitlin abruptly dropped her hand. Simon could see her stiffening, straightening, pulling back.

"I have to go," she said quietly, getting up. She pressed her hand to her cheeks, as if to cool them. She looked away, biting her lip, then turned to him. "I'm sorry Simon, this shouldn't have happened."

How could she say such a thing? That was traditionally his line. "Why not?"

She faced him, her eyes now clouded with sorrow. "I'm a nurse, that's why not. This was a mistake. It's unethical and wrong."

Her words were like repeated douses of cold

water. His feelings for her had been confusing ever since the first moment he saw her, but he would never have called them unethical and wrong.

Because for him, for the first time in his life, what he felt for a woman was pure and decent.

"You better go, then," he said, his voice tight.

She did.

Stop it, Caitlin rebuked herself. Stop thinking about him. She bent over the sink in the ladies' room, splashing cold water on her face, the shock of it clearing her mind. She did it again, and again and again until her cheeks were numb and her fingers stiff.

She dried her face and hands, pausing a moment to look at herself in the mirror again. A wide-eyed, frightened face stared back at her. Her lips looked as if they had been kissed. Puzzled, she lifted a finger to her mouth, wondering what it would be like to have Simon's lips on hers, to feel his strong arms hold her close.

Please help me Lord, she prayed. *I can't have this happen. It's wrong and it doesn't make sense. Please help me stay objective. Help me remember I'm a nurse, a professional who doesn't fall in love with her patients.*

She closed her eyes, took a breath as she felt a peace come over her. *I want to take care of Simon, Lord, but I want to do it the right way. Help me keep my focus. Show me what I should do.* And as she laid it in God's hands she was reminded that she didn't go through life on her own strength. She waited a minute, regaining her composure, then, when she felt her control return, she left.

The ward was quiet when she returned to her desk. It was only nine o'clock, and she had an hour of charting ahead of her. Danielle was on her break and Valerie, one of the other nurses, was just returning to the desk when Caitlin sat down. Thankfully she didn't indulge in any chitchat and Caitlin could get to her work.

Routine, that's what she needed, she thought, pulling out Shane's chart. She clicked the pen when the *ping* of the elevator made her look up. Who would be coming on the ward this time of the night?

The doors of the elevator slid open, and Charles stepped out.

Caitlin felt as if the cold water she had recently splashed on her face shot through her veins. Her throat went dry, and her hands went still.

He stopped just outside the elevator, looking around, his expression puzzled. He saw her then and with a hesitant smile, walked over to where she sat.

"Hello, Caitlin," he said, his deep voice familiar. He came to a stop in front of the high desk, his face and shoulders visible above it. He wore a black topcoat over a navy suit, setting off his blond hair and blue eyes. He was handsome in a clean-cut way.

She only nodded at him, fully aware of the curious stares of Valerie beside her.

"Do you have a few minutes?" he asked quietly.

"I'm kind of busy right now," she replied. She didn't want to spend any more time with him and she was afraid to leave the familiar territory of her desk.

"I brought back your suitcase," he said lifting it slightly so she could see it above the high wall she sat behind.

"Just set it down where you're standing. Thanks." She was surprised how easy it was to keep her tone impersonal.

Charles disappeared as he set it down. When he straightened, he rested his elbows on the desk, leaning closer to her. He glanced sidelong at the nurse sitting beside Caitlin then back. "How have you been?" he asked, his voice lowering.

"I'll just be in the supply room, Caitlin." Valerie pushed her chair back.

Caitlin wanted her to stay. She didn't want to be alone with Charles, not after what just happened in Simon's room. She felt as if her life were spiraling out of control, and the last thing she needed was to face Charles, the man who had started it.

But she said nothing. Charles smiled his thanks then when Valerie was gone, turned back to Caitlin.

"Can we go for coffee, or something?"

"No. I just got off my break." Which I spent

beside the bed of a patient, with Simon, she thought guiltily busying herself with some papers.

"I need to talk to you." Charles's voice held an intensity she had never heard before. She looked up to see his eyes staring down at her, his mouth unsmiling. For the first time she noticed how drawn and tired he looked. Very un-Charles-like.

"What do we have to talk about?" she asked, pulling back from the force of his gaze, unable to stop the touch of sympathy she felt.

"Us. What happened last week. What's going to happen in the future."

"We don't have a future, Charles. I don't know now if we ever did." Caitlin felt intimidated by him towering over her and stood up.

"I made a huge mistake that night. You caught me by surprise."

Caitlin couldn't believe how obtuse he could be. "We've been dating, Charles. Wondering where our relationship is going is hardly a surprise. Moving to Los Angeles, now, *that* was a surprise."

Charles pulled his hand over his face, looking away from her. "I know that, Caitlin. I know all that. It's just that…"

"You've been busy with your career, and I've been busy with mine," she finished for him, crossing her arms over her waist as if in defense. Charles was still attractive, familiar in a comfortable way. But she also knew she never cared for him the way she should have. "We've broken up before for the same reasons."

"That's true, Caitlin, but you know—" he looked back at her, leaning even closer "—I got the promotion I had been wanting for years. Now I have it and I don't have you. I don't know if I came out ahead."

"Are you saying you miss me?"

He sighed as he rubbed his forehead with one finger. "I'm saying I want to try again. I know I haven't always been as attentive as I should and I'm hoping we could find a new footing for our relationship."

Caitlin heard him and knew that beneath the vague words, he still cared for her. He looked up, his expression pained and it hurt her to see him like this.

"I'd like to try again, Caitlin. I know we have a good relationship, we share a common faith, we have the same interests. Please."

"And what about Los Angeles?"

Charles bit his lip. "I'm still going."

Caitlin nodded. "Come, I'll walk with you to the elevator." They were silent until they came to the shining doors. Caitlin turned to him, unable to prevent herself from comparing him to Simon.

"I know it won't work, Charles," she said softly, lifting one shoulder in a negligent shrug. "This isn't the first time we've had to analyze the relationship. Nor is it the first time we've broken up." She softened her words with a smile. "But this time it's for good. Goodbye, Charles," was all she said.

He stared at her a moment, then turned and left.

Caitlin pressed her hand against her chest, but her heart beat steady and sure, her breathing was regular, pulse moderate. Her old boyfriend had stopped by to see her, had asked her for another chance and she didn't really feel any different.

No passion here, she thought with a vague disappointment, remembering what both her mother and sister had said about her. Maybe it was a genetic disorder. Maybe rapture and thrills were not part and parcel of her relationships.

"That your boyfriend?" Valerie asked, finally daring to make an appearance. "He's a honey."

Caitlin sat down, staring sightlessly at the notes pinned on the board in front of her, easily recalling Charles's blue eyes, blond hair styled to perfection. "I suppose," she said vaguely, picking up her pen again.

"What do you mean, you suppose. He's got the good looks of a male model."

Caitlin only shrugged. She knew that when she and Charles first went out, she was attracted to his looks, but over time his face simply became familiar, as did his personality.

Now, he wanted her back and she knew she couldn't be with a man whose touch did nothing to her.

Nothing compared to what happened when Simon had placed his hand on her cheek just minutes ago.

Caitlin bit her lip at the memory. Tried to eradicate pictures of Simon's face, his eyes, the memory of how he had made her feel with that simple touch, wondering why only thoughts of him could do more to her heart than actually seeing Charles did.

Simon stared ahead, listening to voices outside his room. Sound carried so well in this hospital. He often heard the nurses chatting, not realizing how well he could often understand what they were saying.

He had heard the nurses talking about what a difficult patient he was, usually in exasperated tones. He heard them talk about what they were going to be doing when they got off work. He could recognize Danielle's rough voice, Tina's shrill one. Knew that a nurse named Valerie was working tonight and that she thought Caitlin's boyfriend was attractive.

You're a fool, Simon, he berated himself. You should have known that someone like her would have a boyfriend.

He remembered the sound of the guy's voice as he talked with Caitlin. Simon only heard snatches of the conversation but enough to know they had planned a date.

He didn't know why he should care. Caitlin was merely a distraction. He was bored and out of sorts and what he felt toward her was gratitude, nothing more.

He shifted his weight, riding out the pain that accompanied the movement. This morning the physiotherapist had him up on crutches, putting what he called "feather" weight on his leg. He had felt dizzy, but it passed. When Caitlin had said he would be discharged in a couple of weeks, he hadn't believed her, but each day he progressed a little further and he knew it would come.

He was looking forward to leaving. He needed to get out of this room, away from this hospital. In the past few days he had spent too much time thinking about things he had managed to avoid.

Jake, his mother, the lack of family in his life.

Caitlin.

He remembered too vividly the softness of her cheek, how her fingers felt against his. He liked the sound of her voice and too often, when he was bored and lonely, yearned to hear her talking to him.

He found himself wishing she worked the day shift so he could see her more, then thankful she worked the night shift when it was quieter and she could spend some time with him.

He had spent half of today trying to reason his way past how he felt about her, wondering what he meant to her.

He pushed himself over with his elbow, ignoring the pain that accompanied the movement and wishing he could forget Caitlin Severn.

Tonight he had touched her, she had touched him. He had discovered feelings he never knew he possessed. A tenderness of emotion, a caring that passed beyond a physical attraction.

He needed her and even as the thought had bothered him, it gave him a peculiar ache that wasn't unwelcome.

Then after being told that the pure and tender emotions he felt for her were unethical, he found out she had a boyfriend.

He had to quit thinking, that's what he had to do. He never spent this much time sitting around. He was far more accustomed to spending his day on the phone, reading reports, investigating hot leads, analyzing data, running around until it was time to either find a date, or go to bed.

One of the day nurses had brought him a book, an action-adventure thriller. He figured he may as well read it now. It would be just what he needed to get his mind off a nurse who prayed, for goodness sakes.

He heard Shane snoring quietly and without thinking, rolled over to turn on his light. The quick movement sent shattering pain down his leg. He waited until it eased then reached farther to take the book he had been reading off his night table.

He opened it, turned a few pages to find his spot. The words flowed past his eyes, black lines and circles on paper that were supposed to take him away from this hospital, push aside the thoughts that circled in his mind, tormenting him and teasing him.

His mind returned back to his brother, wondering once again where he was, what he was doing. Wondering if Jake regretted not leaving with him that day Simon had called him from a pay phone.

Simon wondered about his mother and where she was, if she was even still alive.

He turned back a page, trying again to read words he had just finished. Concentrating, he managed to pull himself into the story; then he heard Caitlin's voice, and his heart missed its next beat.

He glared past the curtain to the open door.

"Simon, do you need anything?" Caitlin stopped at the foot of his bed, her hands resting on the rail. Her smile was hesitant, appealing and Simon reminded himself of what she had said only a few moments ago. He reminded himself of the boyfriend. Time to retreat.

He forced himself to look back down at the book. "Nothing you can give me, sweetie."

"I'll be in later to check your dressings. The day nurse was concerned about some discharge."

"Can't someone else do it?" he asked, forcing a disinterested tone into his voice. He looked up and curled his lip into a smile. "I wouldn't mind seeing that Valerie again. She's kind of cute."

"I'll tell her you said so," she said, her voice quiet, her face registering no emotion.

"You do that, Caity honey." He winked at her and setting his book down, leaned back, clasping his hands behind his head in what he hoped was a nonchalant pose. Lifting his arm like that made it throb but he refused to let that show. "Or is thinking she's cute, *unethical*." He put a hard emphasis on the last word, hoping it would create some kind of reaction.

"You can think whatever you want, Mr. Steele." Caitlin showed neither by action nor expression that what he said struck home, but as she turned and left, Simon instinctively knew he had hurt her.

It was what he had wanted to do, wasn't it?

Then why did it bother him so much?

Chapter Eight

"Rachel, when you first met Jonathon, what did you feel?" Caitlin asked as she sat on the couch, sipping the hot chocolate her sister had brought her. Caitlin had come home from work, tired and confused. She needed to talk. Thankfully Rachel had been waiting for her.

Rachel smiled, her expression turning dreamy. "Like all the air had been squeezed out of my chest."

Caitlin felt a twinge of jealousy at the emotion in her sister's voice, the breathy sigh at the end. "And when you see him now," she continued, "what do you feel?"

"You know, we can be sitting together in a room and he can look up at me and I can still feel the same thrill."

"Well, I never felt that way with Charles." And I have with Simon.

"Never?"

Caitlin slowly shook her head, setting her cup down on the table in front of her. "Nope. Never."

"A relationship is more than thrills, you know," Rachel said, leaning forward to lay a consoling hand on her sister's arm. "And like I said before, this sure doesn't sound like the Caitlin I know."

"I don't know, Rachel." She pulled her legs under her, laying her head along the back of the couch. "Sometimes when I'm praying, I feel a thrill. When I feel especially close to God, it makes my heart beat faster. I don't think it's unrealistic to expect the same feelings from a relationship with a man."

Rachel held her gaze, then nodded knowingly. "I see what you mean."

Caitlin looked past her sister, remembering another man's touch, the glow of his eyes.

His swaggering attitude.

The clock's resonant *bong* chimed off the hour and Caitlin reluctantly got up, yawning. "I've got to go to bed."

"How many more shifts are you working?"

Caitlin stretched her shoulders back, working a kink out of her neck. "One more night and then I'll be around for a few days. After that it's off to Portland to spend time with Evelyn and Scott."

"Jonathon and I will be here until Monday. We can do something together then."

"Sure." Caitlin bent over and dropped a kiss on her younger sister's head. "I'll see you tomorrow."

She trudged upstairs to the bathroom and had a shower, indulging in a long soak, hoping the hot water would chase away thoughts of mocking eyes, a cocky grin.

A man who could set her heart beating with just a lift of his mouth, the angle of his head. Something her boyfriend of three years couldn't quite manage.

Caitlin closed the door to her bedroom, walked over to the bed and fell backward on it with a *twang* of the bedsprings. She pressed her hands against her face, trying to find equilibrium, a place where she didn't have to do all this thinking and wondering.

Simon.

How easily his face slipped into her mind. His deep-set eyes, the way his hair falls over his forehead, framing his face, the curve of his lips. He has a beautiful mouth.

Too bad he misuses it so often.

Ah, the sharp voice of her own reason, pulling her back to reality. Simon was, as he had said, a blip. He was confusion and frustration and mixed-up emotions all tied in with the reordering of Caitlin's own life. He was a textbook case of the problems encountered with the enforced intimacy between patient and nurse. He was totally out of her league. She knew precious little about him. He didn't share her faith, in fact he often mocked it. He was overbearing and…

And vulnerable and handsome and fascinating in a deep, heart-clenching way that Charles never was.

She knew so little about Simon, his past. The little bits and pieces he threw her were just vague hints. He spoke of a brother, foster parents, an adoptive father, but no mother, no other family. So casually he spoke of his inability to let people get close, as if it were merely a fact of life, not something to deal with.

She got up, and slipped into bed. Yawning, she reached over and picked up her Bible from the nightstand and opened it to the passage she'd been reading. Ecclesiastes. She started reading it a few weeks ago, taking comfort in what she saw as a basic realism, an almost world-weary take on life that suited her own mood.

It put her own problems in perspective and reading it reminded her of something she knew since she was young. She had one basic mandate in life. To love and serve God. Everything else, as the writer said, "was meaningless, chasing after the wind."

But when she got to verse eight of chapter four, she stopped.

Her finger traced the words and as she reread them, they filled her with an eerie sadness. "There was a man all alone; he had neither son nor brother. There was no end to his toil, yet his eyes were not content with his wealth. "For whom am I toiling," he asked, "and why am I depriving myself of enjoyment?"

She placed her fingers on the words, thinking immediately of Simon. How proud he was of his success, that he had done it all on his own. Yet she sensed a sorrow and a loneliness that his money hadn't been able to assuage.

He had no one who missed him, no one who cared enough to visit, to phone or call or send a card or letter.

He was all alone. Like the writer of Ecclesiastes said, he had neither son nor brother. He had money, but no one who mattered to him.

She closed her eyes, laying her head back as she lifted her heart in prayer for him. It was the one time she could think of him and not feel guilty, when she prayed for him.

"Just go slowly now," the physiotherapist urged Simon, "And we'll do this once more."

He nodded, easing his weight to his injured leg. He breathed through the pain.

"Good, you're doing just great," he encouraged, standing close to Simon to support him.

"I'm doing nothing, Trevor," Simon grunted, gripping the crutches.

"Considering you had major surgery to the largest bone in your body almost a week ago, you're doing a lot." Trevor Walton nodded, watching Simon's leg.

"Okay, back onto the bed and we'll work on your other exercises. Tomorrow we'll get you down to the gym for some mat work. Arm over my shoulder now," he instructed, as he easily got Simon onto the bed.

Simon allowed Trevor to help him, much as it galled him. Helplessness was a foreign concept to him. It was something he had fought his whole life. The helplessness of being moved around, of being shifted from home to home. He had vowed he would never be in a situation where he wasn't in control again.

And here he was. In many ways more reliant than he had been as a child. He was completely dependent on people bringing him his food, on helping him in and out of bed. He hadn't been outside for days now and in order to accomplish that, he would have to ask someone.

All day people came in, did something, then left. His bedding got changed, his dressings checked. The day shift was always busy though some of the nurses would take time out to chat with him.

He laughed with them, told them jokes, talked about inane things but none of them caught his fancy enough that it mattered whether they stopped and visited or not.

But it seemed he spent his entire day waiting for the night shift to come on. Waiting for Caitlin to stop by, hoping she had time to talk.

You're nuts, he chastised himself, trying to get comfortable again. Tonight is her last night and then she's finished.

The thought stopped him momentarily. He didn't want to think he might never see her again.

Nor did he want to acknowledge how important she had become to him. He made it a rule with the women he met to keep things at a superficial level. Once he sensed they wanted more, he would leave. But Caitlin had worked herself into his consciousness, into his very being. He wanted to find out more about her, to spend more time with her.

It was her eyes, he figured. Eyes that watched him, watched over him during that first night, eyes that could soften with caring. His heart fluttered as he remembered touching her face yesterday, how she had turned her head into his hand.

When she had called what was building between them unethical, it made him angry. It was the first time in his life he recalled wishing he was a better person. It was the first time in his life that a woman challenged him to do just that.

She's got a boyfriend, idiot. He forced himself to remember that, to recall the date he heard them arrange last night. Caitlin belonged to someone else.

Yet if she did, why did she allow Simon to touch her? Why did he feel so right with her? Why had she stayed?

Well, after your little performance last night she

won't be spending much time with you tonight, he reminded himself, recalling how he had made that ridiculous comment about wanting Valerie to check his dressings.

Simon picked up the action-adventure book he'd begun, forcing his mind back to the story and away from a woman who made him more confused than anyone before.

He read the same page about four times before putting the book down.

Still bored. Bored and confused and his head was busy with thoughts he couldn't seem to still.

Glancing sidelong, he saw the Bible again.

Why not, he thought, reaching for it. He had read it a couple of times since he came here. This time he flipped past the first books of the Old Testament and stopped at Isaiah, not really sure why. He skipped the first part with its woes and imprecations of doom for Israel.

Then he saw it. "Comfort, comfort ye my people." Isaiah 40. The words spoke to a part of him he hadn't wanted to bring out in a long time. Comfort. Who had ever offered him that before? Counselors spoke of owning the problem, of acknowledging his part in what happened in his life, of taking charge and being in control. Foster parents spoke of letting down his guard and allowing people to care.

But other than his adoptive father none of them had offered the comfort he had just read about.

The words were familiar in an old way, he thought, tracing them with his finger. "The voice of one crying in the desert, prepare the way for the Lord." He vaguely remembered hearing them at a church service with candles.

Christmas, he realized as the memory returned. Christmas with Jake and Tom Steele, the widower who'd adopted them. The picture of the three of them sitting in a church pew slipped unbidden into his mind, the soft glow of candlelight as the minister spoke the words of Isaiah 40. The words of promise, of peace, of rest.

Allowing even that small memory to come back created a sharp surge of pain. Simon swallowed, closing his eyes. Weakness, he thought. Dependence. Loss.

He almost threw the book aside, but forced his eyes open, forced himself to get past the pain. He was alone out of choice. Simon pushed his memories aside and read on, determined to get past this.

He got to verse 28 and read, "Do you not know? Have you not heard? The Lord is the everlasting God, the Creator of the ends of the earth. He will not grow tired or weary, and His understanding no one can fathom. He gives strength to the weary and increases the power of the weak. Even youths grow tired and weary, and young men stumble and fall, but those who hope in the Lord will renew their strength. They will soar on wings like eagles; they will run and not grow weary, they will walk and not be faint."

Simon read the words, his heart constricting. He had stumbled and fallen in so many ways. Reading the verses vaguely familiar to him made him look backward to memories he thought he had safely stored away, and by doing so, he compared them to his current life. The decisions he'd made that were so far from the ones he'd been raised to make.

I had no choice, he reiterated to himself. I had to learn to take care of myself. No one else would.

He willed the memories away, laying down the Bible. Mentally he cursed the disability that kept him here in this hospital. He needed to get out, to leave, to keep himself busy.

He needed to outrun the thoughts that plagued him, reminded him of a different life and values.

He didn't want to look at himself anymore. Because when he did, he saw himself through Caitlin's eyes and he didn't like what he saw.

As Caitlin walked up the steps to the ward, she wished she could suppress the sense of expectation that lifted her steps. Much as she liked to deny it, deep within her, she knew it was because of Simon.

His behavior yesterday should have put her off, should have made her realize what kind of guy he was. So why did thoughts of him still make her heart flip?

I'm really going nuts, she thought pushing open the door to the ward. Thank goodness she would be leaving in a few days. She needed to get away, see other places. Balance out the strangeness of her attraction to a patient compared to the lack of emotion she felt around Charles.

Thank goodness it was her last day of work here. Once today was over, Simon would be part of her history.

"Hi girl," Danielle already sat at the desk. "How was yesterday?"

Val piped up from behind the desk, "Her boyfriend stopped by. What a babe."

Danielle gave Caitlin an appraising look. "What did Mr. Frost want?"

Caitlin shrugged, pulling her purse off her shoulder. "To take me out."

"And…" Danielle said.

Thankfully the charge nurse from the previous shift had come to the desk, ending the conversation.

Caitlin checked on a new admission. Vitals had just been done so she would be okay for a while. With a flutter of trepidation, she stepped into Shane and Simon's room. The crowd around Shane's bed was noisy and boisterous. She only recognized Shane's older brother, Matthew, out of the group of mostly teenagers.

"You'll have to keep it down, a bit, I'm afraid,"

Caitlin warned the group with a smile. "There are other patients in this room."

"We can do that," Matthew said with a wink. The girl beside him noticed and turned to give Caitlin an appraising stare that wasn't really friendly. He added, "If there's anything else I can do for you..." He was cut off by an elbow planted in his midsection.

"Give it up, Matt," Shane joked, glancing quickly at Caitlin. "She's got a boyfriend."

Caitlin didn't bother to correct him.

She gave them an inane smile and then stepped around the curtain to face Simon, suppressing a silly schoolgirl flutter at the thought of facing him again.

The light was off above his empty bed, the sheets thrown back.

Her heart stopped, then started again as she noticed a figure by the window, leaning on a pair of crutches.

I never realized he was so tall, she thought. He stood sideways to her. Even in the subdued light from Shane's bed, it wasn't hard to make out his broad shoulders, long legs. He had thrown a hospital-issue dressing gown over his pajamas but even hunched over the crutches, he had a commanding presence.

"Hi, there," she said unable to think of anything else to say. "How did you get out of bed?"

"Determination," he said, still looking out the

window. "What can I do for you?" His voice held the same mocking indifference she had come to associate with him.

"I just came by to see how you're doing. The usual shift-change stuff." She clasped her hands in front of her and lifted them in his direction. "According to Trevor's report, you've been working quite hard today. You should have waited until someone could help you out of bed," she said carefully, striving to keep her voice neutral.

"I had to try myself. I figure the further I progress, the sooner I'm out of here."

It was what she had thought as well, but hearing him articulate it gave it a sense of finality.

"I'll be by later to check on you and help you back into bed. Don't overdo it, okay?"

"You don't have to worry about me, Caitlin," he said quietly, still looking out the window. "I'm sure you don't when you're out of this building."

If only you knew, Caitlin thought. But she wisely said nothing and left.

The evening moved along with painful slowness. Once visiting hours were over a quiet settled onto the ward. Danielle managed to convince Simon to sit in a chair.

Caitlin had checked on the patients after all the visitors had left. Some were sleeping, some were reading.

Simon now sat in his chair, reading, as well.

Caitlin walked closer, her pulse quickening as he looked up at her.

"You should let me help you back into bed," she said, trying to keep her voice steady.

"I've spent too much time in that bed already," he said, looking down again at the book on his lap. With a start Caitlin recognized the Bible from his bedside table.

She wanted to say something, to acknowledge what he read but she felt suddenly tongue-tied and self-conscious.

But he didn't seem to be so afflicted. "So what is it about this book?" he asked, turning a page and looking up at her. "Why am I reading it so much?"

Caitlin took a casual step nearer, encouraged by his questions, the change in his attitude. She wished she could figure him out. "What are you reading?"

Simon looked up with a wry grin. "Isaiah."

"Why did you choose that book?" she asked, surprised. Most people looking for encouragement chose the Psalms.

Simon gave a careful shrug. "I've been going through a bunch of them. Did some of the Psalms, but this fit."

"Fit what?"

"My life." He ran one finger along the gilt edge of the pages, a frown pulling his dark eyebrows together in a scowl. "You know, the wayward, stubborn people."

"But Isaiah holds out hope as well," Caitlin said. "That was the whole purpose of all of the prophets. To point toward the hope of the Messiah, the hope of reconciliation with God."

"The only reconciliation I do is at year end." Simon tilted his head up to her, still frowning. "Did you learn everything you know from Sunday school?"

"Amongst other things." Caitlin recalled the different Bible studies and classes she had attended. "I didn't always enjoy them, but now that I'm older I appreciate the tremendous heritage and wealth of Bible knowledge I've been given by my parents and teachers."

"I went when I was younger," Simon said. "Used to like it."

"Used to…" Caitlin prompted. Simon gave out so little of his past, every bit he handed out made him more real, more accessible.

"Just used to." He said with finality, closing the Bible. Caitlin heard the weariness in his voice.

She knew he would say nothing more tonight so she reverted back to her own job. "According to the physiotherapist, you spent the requisite amount of time sitting. You don't want to overdo it."

"I'll be okay." He shifted his weight and grimaced. "If you don't mind, I'd really like to be alone," he said without looking up. He was pushing her away again, she realized with dismay. He had shown her too much.

"Buzz someone when you want to get back into bed," she said softly, hesitating a moment yet. But Simon said nothing and she left.

Chapter Nine

As Caitlin looked over the inventory in the supply room, she couldn't keep the picture of Simon as he sat in his chair reading the Bible out of her mind. She wondered if he gained any comfort from it, if it made him think. What was he seeking there?

She knew he wouldn't ask. She knew Simon well enough by now to know that, to him, asking was a sign of weakness.

When she was done she glanced at her watch. This was crazy. It didn't matter anymore what he wanted to prove, she had to get him back into bed.

As she passed the desk, she dropped the inventory sheet off and kept walking to Simon's room.

His light was still on and as she came around the curtain dividing the two beds it was to see him staring out the window. The Bible no longer lay on his lap.

He turned his head when she came in and this time, instead of indifference, she saw sorrow.

"How are you doing, Simon?" she asked, her voice quiet.

"I'd like to get back into bed now."

"I'll call Danielle to help."

"No. I got out by myself. I could probably get back in by myself..." his words drifted off and Caitlin wondered what he was going to say. But he kept silent.

"But you're tired now."

He simply nodded and Caitlin took it for acquiescence. "Just put your arm around my shoulder and lean on me when you stand up." Caitlin approached the chair, bending at her knees to take up a position right beside him. Simon laid his arm across her shoulder. "Lean on me and on three we'll stand up." She counted and Simon slowly got up as she straightened. She put her other arm around him, trying to ignore the strength of his muscles and the warmth of his torso through his pajamas, the thin hospital gown. "Now take a few short steps backward to your bed."

Simon didn't move and Caitlin looked up at him, puzzled.

His dark eyes glittered down at her and as she watched, he shifted his weight to his good leg, turning to face her.

"What are you doing?" she asked, her voice suddenly breathless as, for the first time since she met him, she looked up at him. She had to tilt her head back to do so.

"Something I've been wondering about for too long." His other arm came around her waist to hold her close to him and then, as Caitlin watched, mesmerized, he lowered his head. In a last, futile effort to keep her sanity, she kept her eyes open when his mouth touched hers. Then as his lips moved softly, gently, she felt her eyes drift closed, all coherent thought fled. There was only him, and the strength and warmth of his arms, his mouth on hers.

He was the first to draw away, resting his forehead against hers as he drew in a ragged breath. "What are you doing to me, angel?"

Caitlin felt as if all her breath had slowly been pressed out of her chest. She tried to take a breath, tried to force herself to move, but all she wanted was to be held by Simon, to stay in this place where time had ceased to exist, where she was no longer a nurse and he no longer a patient.

"I used to know what I wanted," he said, his breath teasing her hair as he touched his lips to her temple. "I thought I didn't need anything. Now you've got me all mixed up, reading the Bible, finding out what a scoundrel I really am…." He kissed her hair, a light touch of his mouth.

Caitlin heard his words, felt a surge of hope at his doubts. But her practical nature took over and she carefully drew back. "You have to let me go, Simon," she whispered.

His chest lifted in a sigh and he pressed her head in the lee of his neck. "No. I don't want to."

"Please, Simon." She didn't dare shift her weight for fear he'd fall. She wished she had asked Danielle to help.

He raised his head, as he let one arm drop to his side. The other still lay heavily across her shoulder. For a moment they stood, facing each other, unasked questions keeping her from taking that small step closer to him to lessen the distance.

Why did you do that? What do I mean to you? What am I doing? The questions tripped over themselves with no answer coming.

He was all wrong for her. He was a dangerous unknown, a lost, lonely soul.

"Caitlin, what's wrong?"

"Nothing's wrong," she lied, ignoring the tripping of her heart, the breath that refused to return to her lungs. She resisted the urge to run away, to flee.

He shook his head as he reached for her, sliding one rough finger down her cheek. "How do you manage to turn your emotions off so quickly?" he asked, tilting his head to one side to look at her.

"Simon, please. It's late, and you need to get back into bed."

"I'm safer there, aren't I Caitlin? I can't reach you there."

She didn't want to listen, to know he was partially right. She didn't want to admit that he frightened her.

"Once I'm lying down you're in charge," he continued. "You can keep me at a distance. You can fool yourself into thinking just like I've tried to do that what's happening between us will simply go away once you leave this hospital and you can go back to Charles." As he took a step nearer he swayed slightly and Caitlin instinctively reached out to catch him.

Once again his arms were around her. Once again his mouth sought hers. As they met, he stifled her cry of protest. He held her tight against him, his arms strong, protective, his mouth insistent. He pulled away, a grin lifting the corner of his mouth. His expression was triumphant.

She didn't like the look on his face and forced his arms down. "Stop it, now. I don't care what you think, I don't care how you see me. This is wrong, and you can't make it right just by force of your will." She didn't want to look at him, didn't want to acknowledge the emotional hold he had over her. "What's happening between us is nothing new. Once you're gone, you'll forget all about me and the same will happen to me."

"And you can go back to Charles?" he said with a sneer.

Caitlin's heart flipped but she forced herself to concentrate, to remind herself that he was her patient, that she had a job to do. "My personal life is none of your concern." She drew in a slow breath as she prayed for equilibrium, for strength, for wisdom. "And now, I'm going to ask you once again to let me help you back into bed."

Simon stayed where he was, as if measuring her strength, then with a shrug, turned.

"Wait a minute, Simon," she warned.

But he moved too quickly. He didn't get his injured leg around soon enough to bear the weight. He threw out his arms just as Caitlin rushed forward.

Simon let out a harsh, loud cry as his leg twisted. She caught him, but his momentum combined with his weight was too much for her to hold up.

Caitlin managed to turn him so that he fell on top of her instead of the floor. She felt her breath leave her as they landed with a crash.

Stars and electrical impulses shot through her head, followed by a jolt of pain. Above her, Simon cried out again and she could do nothing. He was a dead weight.

She heard the squeak of rubber-soled shoes as thankfully, someone rushed into the room.

"What happened?" Caitlin heard Danielle's voice and then Simon was carefully rolled off of her.

"He moved too quickly," Caitlin said, her voice groggy with pain. "Then he fell. I couldn't stop him."

"Simon, Simon can you hear me?" Danielle

was crouched over Simon's inert body, checking him over.

"Where's Caitlin?" he called out, his eyes shut against the agony Caitlin knew must be coursing through his body. "Is she okay?"

"I'm okay," she said. She could get up, but her head was spinning and she couldn't seem to focus on what was happening.

"What about you, Simon? How's your leg?"

"Hurts," he whispered tightly.

Another nurse, Eva, came running into the room as Caitlin slowly got to her feet.

"Page the resident, Dr. Foth. Get him down here stat." Danielle said.

Eva ran out of the room leaving Caitlin and Danielle with Simon.

Simon's cries cut through Caitlin. Sweat broke out on his forehead, and he was clenching his teeth.

"He's going to need an X ray," Danielle said, holding Simon's head. Caitlin only nodded, her head spinning.

Thankfully they didn't have long to wait. Dr. Foth came immediately, Eva right behind him pushing a gurney. Dr. Foth checked him over and ordered him to be taken immediately to X ray.

"We need to make sure there's been no damage to that plate." He shook his head as he got up.

Hating her ineffectiveness, Caitlin managed to work her way around to the other side of the gurney, pushing it closer to Danielle, Dr. Foth and Eva. As they carefully lifted Simon on it, he cried out again, a harsh sound in the usual quiet of the night.

He lay panting, his eyes closed, his hands clenching the sheets at his sides. Each breath came out on a whimper that tore at her heart. Head spinning, Caitlin had to force herself to focus, to concentrate as she stepped closer to him. She had to touch him, to let him know she was there.

"Angel," he breathed, when he opened his eyes and saw her. "I hurt you."

"No. Just relax now." Talking was an effort but she needed to reassure him, to ease his own suffering. *Please Lord, let his leg be all right. Please don't let anything serious have happened to him,* she prayed, touching his arm, connecting with him.

She felt Eva take her arm and resisted. She didn't want to leave until she knew he was okay.

"Danielle and the doctor will take him down," Eva said, gently drawing her away from Simon's side. "You should get checked over, too. You don't look too good."

"I'm okay," she lied, straightening and walking slowly out of the room.

I hope they take good care of him, Caitlin thought as she watched the elevator doors slide behind them.

She blinked slowly, swaying as the lights above her seemed to dim. Then the desk in front of her tilted, spun then receded down a long black corridor.

* * *

"Are you sure you should be up and about?" Rachel asked from the bottom of the stairs.

"I'm okay," Caitlin protested, her head pounding ferociously with each step. "I'm sick of lying around."

"Here, let me help you." Rachel held out her arm.

"I'll be okay," Caitlin said, ignoring her sister's help. She misjudged the last step, and the jolt of hitting the floor too hard sent pain slicing behind her eyes.

"Don't be so stubborn, Caitlin. What if all your patients acted like you do?"

I already have one who does, Caitlin thought. She realized her folly and leaned on her sister's arm, grateful for the help.

"We're just going to start lunch." Rachel brought her down the hallway to the kitchen.

Caitlin's mother got up. "Oh, honey. You should still be in bed."

"I'm fine Mom. It's just a concussion."

It wasn't "just" a concussion and Caitlin knew that. She had experienced a loss of consciousness. After being checked over by a neurologist she was ordered home to bed. After lying around for a day, she knew exactly why Simon had been so irritable. In fact, she gave him a lot of credit for not being even worse than he was.

Her mother pulled out a chair for her. "Sit down then and have something to eat. You're so pale."

Caitlin obediently sat down, allowed her mother a moment of fussing as she met her father's eyes. He smiled at her over his glasses, but his expression was concerned.

"Let's have a moment of prayer," he said as they all bowed their heads.

Caitlin heard her father's familiar voice as he prayed, his tone familiar, as if he were addressing a well-respected friend. She heard the words of his prayer as he asked for a blessing on the food, a blessing on each of their children, healing for Caitlin, strength for Jonathon and Rachel, and Evelyn and Scott in Portland. He didn't mention Tony by name this time, but each family member present echoed his unspoken words. Before raising her head at the end of his prayer, Caitlin sent up her own prayer for Simon, that he didn't suffer any major injury from his fall.

Her own head still throbbed, but it was a bearable pain. She knew that by tomorrow it would be gone.

"I made some chicken soup, Caitlin. I know it's your favorite." Jean handed her a bowl of steaming broth, with thick egg noodles and chunks of chicken floating in it.

"Smells and looks delicious." Caitlin smiled her thanks up at her mother as she took the bowl.

Soon everyone was eating, the conversation desultory.

"So, what exactly happened to you, Caitlin?" Rachel asked, turning to her sister.

"I was helping a patient into bed and we fell," Caitlin said simply.

"And how's the patient?"

"I don't know. I was hoping to phone the hospital once I felt a little better."

"I always told you, one day you'd fall for a patient," her father teased.

Caitlin couldn't stop the blush that warmed her neck and crept up her cheeks.

After lunch, the rest of the day slipped by. Caitlin napped, tried to watch television and tried not to think about Simon.

She and Rachel sat out in the backyard for a while, but the rain and wind soon sent them back inside again. They ended up in Caitlin's room, sorting through old pictures. Rachel wanted to make up a photo album for her future child.

"Oh, look. This is a cute one of the two of us." Rachel leaned sideways, tilting a photograph of Caitlin and Rachel dressed in identical bathing suits. "This was taken at Long Beach, over twenty years ago."

Caitlin obediently looked and smiled. She couldn't get excited about pictures from the past when her future seemed to loom ahead of her uncertain and vague.

She didn't know in which neat compartment of her life to put Simon. He was unsuitable in so many ways. His past was a question, and he didn't care about the future. He seemed to be searching, yet wouldn't admit that to anyone.

He didn't profess to believe in or hold the same values she did, yet she sensed that he had been raised with them. He read the Bible, yet didn't want to talk about it.

She recalled the look of confusion and yearning on his face yesterday as he sat in the chair, the Bible on his lap. He looked defenseless and once again she was drawn to him.

"...one of the only times I saw you really angry."

Caitlin blinked, pulling herself back to the here and now. She glanced sidelong at Rachel, wondering if her sister had noticed her lapse.

Rachel was looking directly at her. "I don't think it's the concussion that put that dreamy look on your face, Caitlin." She set the box of old pictures aside and turned to sit cross-legged on the bed, facing Caitlin. "What's been happening at work, Caitlin? You didn't say much the other night when I waited up for you, but I could tell something's been going on."

Caitlin frowned, pretending not to understand. She had spoken to Danielle about Simon, but only in the vaguest terms. She wouldn't get away with that with her sister, but at the same time she wasn't sure she wanted to pull out and examine such new and fresh feelings. Feelings that were confusing and frightening.

"You've met someone, haven't you?" Rachel said quietly, leaning her elbows on her knees.

Caitlin leaned back against the headboard. "Yes," she replied softly. "Yes, I have."

"And..." Rachel prompted.

"And what?"

"Does he make your heart do those painfully slow flips when you see him? When your eyes meet, does it feel like you might never breathe again? Does he give you that thrill you've been looking for?"

Caitlin could only nod, feeling that very sensation right now. "Yes, he does," she said, thinking of Simon's dark hazel eyes that could tease and challenge at one time and yet show glimpses of vulnerability and need.

"Who is he? Do I know him?" Rachel leaned forward, grabbing her sister's hands. "How come you never mentioned him before? Is he the reason you broke up with Charles?"

Caitlin met her sister's excited gaze and debated the wisdom of telling her. It would make something that she thought of as nebulous, real and the thought frightened her.

"No, you don't know him," Caitlin said, adding with a short laugh, "I barely know him."

"What do you mean?"

Caitlin pulled her hands free from her sister's, folding her arms across her chest. "He's a patient in the hospital."

Rachel's one eyebrow shot up and she tilted her head sideways as if inspecting a person who had mysteriously taken the place of her sister. "A patient?" she asked, incredulous.

"You don't have to act as if it's evil, for goodness sakes. Happens often," Caitlin replied, a defensive tone creeping into her voice.

"I know that. But I remember how you used to talk about the nurses it happened to...." Rachel's voice trailed off. "You used to get so angry at them."

"Well, maybe the Lord figured I needed some humbling," Caitlin said, her shoulders lifting in a sigh. "Believe me, I've fought it myself. I don't even know if what I'm feeling is really what I'm feeling, or if it's just rebound. The circumstances are a little extenuating. I was at the scene of the accident where he was injured."

"The one that you talked about? The motorcycle accident?"

Caitlin nodded. "He was in really rough shape. Broke his femur, a very major and life-threatening injury. I was at the scene, my hand on his pulse. I could feel him slowly drifting away. I'm sure he was dying, Rachel. Right in front of my eyes. I started praying and then his pulse came back. I still get the shivers when I think about it. He claims I saved his life. He wouldn't let me go, kept asking for me in spite of the pain he was in." Caitlin drew in a steadying breath, holding her sister's surprised gaze.

Rachel puffed up her cheeks and slowly released her breath. "Wow, Caity. That's quite dramatic."

"I know. I'm wondering if that's part of the problem."

"What's his name?"

Caitlin let out a short laugh. "It's Simon. From the precious little he's told me, he was raised in a variety of foster homes. He ran away from the last one at age sixteen."

"If I didn't know you as well as I do, I would say that what you feel for him is a type of misplaced mothering syndrome. But you're not the type, Caity." Rachel traced the pattern on the quilt, looking down. "It sounds like he's had a pretty rough life…." Rachel's voice trailed off and Caitlin could hear the unspoken question in it.

"I'm not going to marry him, for goodness sakes." Caitlin said. "I don't know what's happening between us, if anything." She lifted her hands in a helpless gesture. "I have to admit he's very appealing and he makes me feel…"

"Weak in the knees."

Caitlin laughed shortly. "Yeah. Pretty much. I

suppose it's just a physical thing, yet sometimes there's more. I've caught him reading the Bible, but one of the first things he told me was that praying was a waste of time."

"Cynical, then."

"Big time." Caitlin frowned. "Yet, I see in him a searching. He as much as said he won't let people close."

"How does he feel about you?"

"I wish I knew. He claims something is happening between us and at the same time he pushes me away."

"Defense mechanism." Rachel rested her elbows on her knees, her chin on her hands. "He sounds the complete opposite of Charles, maybe it's like you said—a type of rebound thing."

Caitlin shook her head, then winced. "But you know what? When I saw Charles again, I realized there was something missing. More than just how Simon makes me feel..." She paused, thinking of Simon, remembering her last evening with him, how his arms felt around her, his mouth on hers, remembering him reading the Bible, his questions. She and Charles had always made assumptions about their faith. They never spoke much of it. But Simon's questions showed her a man who, in spite of his own bravado, still wasn't afraid to show his own weakness.

She didn't know Charles's weaknesses, she thought.

"You're going dreamy again, sis," Rachel waved a

hand in front of Caitlin's face. "Suitable or not suitable, you've got it bad."

Caitlin blinked. "Maybe I do," she said, sighing lightly. "I just know that for the first time in my life, I *don't* know what to do." Caitlin closed her eyes, her head throbbing. "Maybe it's just this concussion that's got me all confused." But even as she said that, Caitlin knew it wasn't true. Simon had her befuddled long before this.

"Caitlin, you have never known any other boyfriend but Charles. This Simon guy sounds like trouble, yet when you talk about him I see a hint of that passion you were talking about. I think you care for him and I don't think that's so wrong. Don't worry about it Caitlin. Pray about it. God will work His perfect and pleasing will, whatever that may be." Rachel gave her sister a hug.

Caitlin returned the hug, comforted by what her sister said, realizing that no matter how many times she heard the phrase, it was true.

"And I'll expect a progress report when we come back for Mom's birthday," Rachel said with a wink.

Chapter Ten

It was just like before. Dim sounds. Snatches of conversation. Unknown. Unable to understand.

Simon struggled to open his eyes, his head pounding but he couldn't focus.

"Caitlin," he called out involuntarily, then stopped himself. Why did he always want her? What made him call out for her?

"It's okay, Simon," he heard. But it wasn't Caitlin. He tried to turn his head in the direction of the voice, tried to focus.

"Who are you?" he croaked. "What's wrong with me?"

"Danielle. I'm the evening nurse. You've got a bad case of the flu. Do you want a drink?"

"No. Where's Caitlin?" he couldn't help asking.

"She's not working."

As her words registered, a sudden panic pressed

down on him. "She's supposed to come. She said she'd stay."

"Lie still or you'll be in trouble again."

"No, I can't...." Part of his mind registered his incoherence, yet he couldn't stop the agitation that gripped him. His thoughts spun around his head. He couldn't pin them down, couldn't catch them. All he knew was that he wanted Caitlin beside him. He wanted to tell her...to tell her...

He closed his eyes as a wave of vertigo washed away the words. He drifted away, his eyes burning, his leg on fire.

Time was nothing. There was no way to measure what was happening. Nothing made any sense.

He thought he saw Jake standing beside the bed but Jake didn't know he was here, did he? He tried to reach out for him, but his brother slowly disappeared. He heard voices, laughing, mocking. Sounds amplified and confusion reigned.

He was afraid, alone, wandering through darkness, pushing aside hands that held, that pulled on him, trying to find a brother who was always out of his reach. How could Jake turn his back on him? How could he so easily forget him? Everyone had forgotten him. Everyone.

My son, pay attention.... You are my son.... This is my beloved son...my son, give me your heart....

Words slipped through his delirium. Words from

a father to a son. Words he realized came from the Bible.

He didn't want to remember them. He wasn't anyone's son, but the words echoed, words of love.

Such a weak word, *love*. So overused and overrated.

He didn't want to think about love. Didn't want to think about being a son, having a father, a brother. He wished he could stop his thoughts, he wished he could control them. Hearing voices happened to crazy people.

"He's been like this for most of today."

More voices, but these came from outside. Real voices.

"He's really spiked a temp." Caitlin's voice. He was sure of it. He tried to open his eyes but the light was too harsh. "Infection?" he heard her ask.

"No. Blood work shows nothing. It's that flu that's been going around."

"I'll stay with him. You can go back to work."

Then through the heat and confusion he felt a cool touch on his forehead, a click as the light above his bed was turned down a notch. He didn't know if he imagined the gentle touch of lips on his cheek.

"Simon, I'm here."

He felt a soft peace drift over him at the sound of her voice. "Angel," he whispered, thankfully. He could finally open his eyes without a sharp pain from the light hitting him behind his eyes.

And there she was. Leaning above him, her hair framing her face, as she gently smoothed his own hair back from his forehead. "You came," he said.

She nodded, as she let her hand linger on his cheek. He smiled back at her and tried to lick his lips. They were dry and cracked.

"I'll get you a drink," she said, straightening. He heard the clatter of ice and water being poured into a plastic cup, then her hand was behind his head again and she was helping him to drink.

The water was cool, soothing. When he was done he looked up at her, remembering with a sudden clarity what he had done the last time they saw each other. He remembered that he had hurt her then.

"Caitlin, I'm sorry." He forced the words past his own resistance. He wanted to touch her, to connect with her but it seemed each time he did it wrong. "I'm sorry I hurt you. I'm sorry I kissed you...." he tried to find the right words to do something he wasn't very good at. Apologizing.

"No, Simon, don't say that." She sat down beside him, the chair pulled up close.

"Are you going to stay with me?"

She nodded, laughing shortly. "Yes, it seems that is to be my fate. Holding your hand through your various crises."

He smiled weakly, then closed his eyes again. Unorganized thoughts were coming back, spinning around, sucking him down.

"Caitlin," he whispered.

"What, Simon?"

"Pray for me."

"I always do," she replied. "Now just rest. I'm here."

And that knowledge made it easier for him to sleep.

The dreams came anyhow. Unbidden and unorganized—a jumble of memories and people from his past and present melding, accusing. Verses from Bible passages he read condemned him, his life-style. In his dreams he tried to run away, to leave the voices behind him, but they always found him, circling, attacking. He tried to beat them off but couldn't. There were too many—old girlfriends that he walked away from without a second glance, foster parents he left with a shrug, people he had ignored. Jake. His brother, his only brother.

They all hovered and tormented...

"Comfort, comfort my people, says your God."

There were those words again. Simon strained toward them, reaching out. Caitlin was reading, her voice an anchor, the words soothing. "Speak tenderly to Jerusalem, and proclaim to her that her hard service has been completed, that her sin has been paid for, that she has received from the Lord's hand double for all her sins."

Simon heard the words of assurance, the same

words he had read only a few days ago. They gently brushed away the confusion.

Paid for, Caitlin had read. Hard service completed, sin paid for. It sounded too easy.

Simon opened his eyes. The first thing he saw was Caitlin's bent head. She was still reading aloud, her voice resonant with conviction. She glanced up as she turned a page and met his gaze with her own.

"Hi," she said with a hesitant smile. "You were so restless, I thought I would read for you." She held up the Bible. "You had a bookmark in this section. Isaiah 55."

Simon felt a blessed moment of coherence. "Yeah," he said with a short laugh. "Thought it was appropriate, considering where I've been."

Caitlin lowered the Bible to her lap. "And where was that?"

Simon heard the concern in her voice and once again wondered at this woman. Wondered why she willingly spent time with him in spite of what he had said and done to her.

"If you don't want to talk about it I understand."

He shook his head and smiled. "No. I want to." He drew in a slow breath. "I've been all over and nowhere."

"Where did you start from?"

"Foster home."

"What about before that?"

Simon was quiet, remembering Tom Steele, his

adoptive home and the vague memories he had of a mother before that. He had tried to keep the memories alive but over time they had faded into the dim picture of a smile, dark hair and the faint smell of bread baking. It was all he had left of her, and it was all he had left of Tom Steele, the only father he ever knew. Memories.

"My mother gave me and my brother up when I was four years old. I don't remember much of her."

Caitlin leaned closer. "Do you know why she gave you up?"

"No." His head ached again and he felt a burning pain in his leg. "I wanted to go looking for her but Jake didn't."

"Jake is your brother?"

Simon nodded, turning his head to look back at the ceiling. "We used to visit each other after we got split up. He ended up in a great place."

"And you got split because of your running away?" Caitlin sounded surprised.

"Well, I was the bad boy and Jake was the good boy. Special Services wanted to give him a chance separate from me." He felt the ache behind his eyes and a peculiar pressure building in his chest. "But Jake didn't want to leave. Didn't want to come with me. He made the right choice, I think."

"Where is he now?"

"I don't know." Simon drew in a long breath, surprised at the emotions those few words brought out. Sorrow, regret, pain. In his weakened state he couldn't fight them. Had no defenses to draw from. "When he wouldn't leave with me," he continued, "I told him he'd never hear from me again. And he hasn't."

"Would you want to see him again?"

Simon shrugged, but the movement sent a wave of dizziness over him. "I don't know," he said, suddenly weary. "It's been so long. I don't feel I have the right." He closed his eyes and felt Caitlin lightly lay her cool hand on his forehead.

"You're burning up," she murmured. "I'll see if I can get you something."

She walked out of the room, a shadow in the half light and Simon felt bereft.

How had she done it he wondered. How had this woman managed to so completely take hold of him, invade his thoughts and dreams, make him talk about things he had long buried and tried to forget? Remind him of where he had come from and make him wonder where he was going?

He needed her and didn't want to need her.

Simon forced that thought aside. He couldn't allow those emotions to take over his life, determining what he would do. He had been too long on his own, too long independent. He couldn't afford to lean on anyone, to be weak. Caitlin had the potential to destroy everything he had worked so hard to build. He reminded himself that she was a temporary part of his life. She told him over and over again. She was a Christian, far removed from him. She had a boyfriend. A family—something he knew nothing about.

So why did he feel this way about her? Confused, frustrated. Seeking.

Comfort, comfort my people. Those words again, he thought, clinging to them, remembering that God promised that sins would be paid for. He remembered vague snatches of Sunday school songs, words of promise and hope, but also of responsibility.

He had to confess, to show his need to God, to recognize his part in what had been happening in his life. He had to open himself up, look at what he had done.

He didn't know if he could.

His thoughts circled again and when Caitlin returned he was tired and confused.

"Here," she said, lifting his head again. "Take this."

He obediently swallowed the pill she gave him and laid back. She placed a damp cloth on his forehead and he felt immediate relief.

"That feels good," he murmured. "Thanks."

"You want to sleep?"

"No. Just talk to me." He was tired, but he feared the confusion of his dreams. He wanted to hear her voice, to keep the connection between them, however fragile.

"About…" she prompted.

"Tell me about you."

"I already have," she replied quietly. "You know most everything about me."

Simon turned his head, his eyes blinking slowly. "No, I don't. I don't know your favorite color, what you like to do when you're not holding my hand, what you order in a restaurant?"

"I like the color blue, I read books in my spare time and I always order chicken." She fussed with his sheets, her fingers lingering on his shoulder. "Now rest."

Simon laughed shortly. "That was supposed to be the start of a longer conversation." His head ached and his body felt as if it were slowly being pulled in different directions. He should be sleeping, but he had Caitlin all to himself. She wasn't going to rush off to be with another patient, she wasn't here as a nurse, but as a visitor.

He didn't want to speculate on the reasons she was at his side. He was thankful for her presence and for the moment he just wanted to enjoy having her undivided attention.

"I could ask you a few questions," she said.

"You already have."

"These will be simpler. Your favorite color."

"Brown."

"Favorite food."

"French fries."

"Hobbies?"

Simon paused. "I don't know. I keep pretty busy with my work."

"Which is?"

"Work. Just work."

"Sounds fishy, Simon." Caitlin leaned back, crossing her arms, her I-mean-business pose.

"I don't know what else to say," he replied defensively. "I'm self-employed. I buy and sell stocks and businesses and real estate. I have a couple of fast-food franchises, a soft-drink franchise. I manage my own funds…." He stopped, looking at her, trying to read her expression, feeling as if he had to justify what he did. "It's not your usual nine-to-five, pack-a-lunch job. I worked enough for other people, spent enough of my life trying to rise up to other people's expectations and failing…." He stopped again, realizing he had said more than he had wanted to.

"Do you mean the foster homes you lived in?"

Simon said nothing, as a band of sorrow squeezed his heart into a tight knot.

"You said your mother gave you up when you were four," Caitlin persisted.

"You said easy questions," Simon said trying to smile.

"Sorry." She leaned forward. "I can't help it. I want to know more about you. More than you're telling me."

Simon met her eyes and once again felt as if he

were falling. He closed his eyes and took a few deep breaths. "When my mom gave us up we were brought to a foster home. The man was an older man. A widower. We were only supposed to be there temporarily, while we waited for an adoptive home. It took a little longer than Social Services thought it would. He got attached and adopted us. He took care of us until we turned twelve. Then we were moved."

"How come?"

Simon clutched the bed sheet as he stared sightlessly up at the ceiling tiles. "It wasn't because of our father. Tom Steele was a good man. He took us to church, taught us about God. He took us to hockey games, came to parent-teacher interviews. Did all the right things." Simon stopped, untangled his hand from the sheet and closed his eyes.

"What happened?"

Caitlin wouldn't let up, he thought. Her soft-spoken questions slowly kept him going back to places he had thought he had long abandoned.

He drew in a deep breath, swallowing. Sixteen years had passed and dredging up this memory still hurt.

"He died." He ignored Caitlin's cry of dismay. "And Jake and I were moved." He waited a moment, letting the pain pass. "Jake seemed to take it better than me. I couldn't take it at all. So I ran away. I said it was to find my mother. The home they moved us to couldn't handle it so Social Services moved us

again. I kept running. And we were moved again."
He stopped.

"What happened at that time?" she said, her voice
quietly persistent.

"Jake went to stay on a farm in the country and I
ended up in a treatment foster home. But I kept running."

"Why?"

The question was simple enough but it required so
much. He didn't want to analyze his past. It was over.
There was nothing he could do about it. But against
his rational judgment, he wanted her to know all
about him. Wanted her to see what his life was like.
That way, if she stayed then it meant…it meant…

"I'm sorry," she said quietly. "I'm getting nosy."

"No," he replied, looking back up at the ceiling.
"That's okay." He went back through his memories,
digging up old emotions, realizing he was laying
himself bare for her. But he didn't want to analyze,
to defend, to hold back. He wanted her to know. "I
hated everyone for a long time. I hated my mother
for giving us up. I hated Tom Steele for dying and
leaving us. I never knew what to do with the emotions. The first home we were moved to was a good
place, but I never gave it a chance. I didn't want to.
I figured the only way I would be in charge was if I
was the first one to leave. The family kept coming
after me and finally they couldn't handle it anymore.
So Jake and I got moved. And the same thing hap-

pened. Finally we were split up. Jake hated me for a while. I hated him. He ended up in a good place, and I ended up in a sterner home. So I kept running. I suppose by that time it was just a habit, a way of avoiding life."

"And where is Jake now?"

Simon shrugged. "I don't know. Once kids in foster care turn eighteen, they're on their own. I figured he left there, too!"

"Have you ever tried to contact him?"

"No."

"Why not?"

Simon felt it again. Regret, hurt pride. "I don't know if he'd want to hear from me."

"But he's your brother."

Simon shook his head slowly. "Family doesn't work the same for me as it does for you. We've been apart longer than we've been together. He's got his own life. He doesn't need me."

Simon stopped, reaching up to touch his forehead.

Caitlin got up right away, took the now warm cloth off his forehead and replaced it with another. She gently smoothed it against his head, her fingers lingering at his temple, stroking his damp hair back. He saw pity on her face.

He caught her hand, squeezing it hard. "Don't do that, Caitlin," he said, his voice low. "Don't feel sorry for me."

She only smiled, turning her hand in his to curve around his fingers.

"That's not what I want from you."

"That's not what I feel for you," she whispered.

Caitlin's eyes met his, held, and Simon felt his breath leave his chest.

Then she bent forward, touching her lips to his cheek. Her mouth lingered a moment, then she raised her head, clutching his hand.

"What am I going to do with you, Simon?" she asked.

He didn't answer, only held her gaze with his own, yearning and fighting at the same time. He felt a fear grip him at the feelings she evoked in him, the vulnerability she was creating. But he knew that for now, he needed her. "Just stay here, okay?"

She nodded and gently touched his eyelids. "Go to sleep now," she said, her voice quiet, weary.

He kept his eyes closed and clutched her hand as he slowly slipped away into a dreamless sleep.

Caitlin yawned and stretched her arms in front of her.

The light above Simon's bed reflected off the ceiling, creating a soft glow, a soft intimacy.

Beyond the drawn curtain, the bed was empty. Shane had left this morning.

Déjà vu all over again, Caitlin thought remembering another evening, sitting at Simon's bedside.

Except this time she was dressed more for the part with sensible shoes and pants. This time she came out of choice.

And this time she couldn't keep her eyes off Simon's face, couldn't keep herself from touching him, connecting with him however she could. In sleep he looked defenseless, his features relaxed, the parenthetical frown between his eyebrows eased. His mouth lost its cynical twist, softened and curved into a gentle smile.

Caitlin tried to reason out her attraction to him, hoping that by doing so she could deal with it and maybe, understand it.

Simon wasn't as handsome as Charles, she thought, her eyes traveling over his face. He didn't have the classical profile or the even features. If she was to be honest, his nose was a little large, his eyes deep set, yet as she looked at him she felt a yearning, a need to touch him, to comfort him. Thinking of his eyes made her heart give a silly jump. Thinking of his kiss made her jittery.

All the things Charles had never made her feel.

Caitlin knew it wasn't enough to build a relationship on. As Rachel had said, maybe it was merely rebound. Maybe once she was in Portland she would discover that it was Charles she really wanted.

If dating for the rest of your life is what you want, she thought wryly. And that was the harsh reality of going out with Charles. That and moving to L.A.

What kind of relationship did we have she wondered, leaning back in the chair. We dated for three years. I'm apart from him a couple of weeks and I easily forget him.

She slouched down in the chair, opening the Bible. As she flipped through the pages she stopped to read a few Psalms, then turned to Isaiah, still puzzled as to why Simon had chosen this particular book. She turned to the passage she had read to him just a few moments ago remembering how it had settled him.

He was seeking, she knew that. How close he was, well, that appeared to be another question. Simon didn't answer them very readily.

Help me to understand what I should be feeling, Lord, she prayed. *I want to serve You, I want to do what is pleasing in Your sight. I want to be a faithful child of Yours and I know that any future partner must also be Your child. Otherwise it just doesn't work.*

She knew what happened to relationships where one was a Christian and the other not. She had seen evidence of it over and over again. Even in her own family. She wasn't going to make the same mistake her brother had.

Simon moaned softly and laying the Bible down, Caitlin got up. The cloth she removed from his forehead was warm, attesting to the fever that racked him. She took it to the bathroom sink, soaked it in cold water and when she came back, he was awake. Barely.

He smiled at her, his eyes blinking slowly. "Dear Caitlin," he whispered as she laid the cool cloth carefully on his forehead again.

He watched her as she carefully wiped away the excess water that ran in a rivulet down the side of his head. She tried to ignore him, tried not to answer the gentle summons of his gaze.

But she couldn't. As their eyes met, she felt her heart lift. Then he smiled once again, and drifted back off to sleep.

Caitlin watched him a moment, then shaking her head, sat down in the chair again.

Chapter Eleven

"Simon." The soft voice slowly pierced his sleep, a warm hand held his shoulder. Caitlin, Simon thought.

"Hi," he said, focusing on her face. "You're here."

Caitlin nodded pulling her hand away from him. "How are you feeling?"

"Much better." He blinked, and looked around testing his vision. "A lot better."

"Your fever is down." She straightened his blankets, her hand lingering on his arm. "You slept pretty deep."

"Sorry, I would have preferred to talk to you." He didn't know how long he slept, but even if it was only an hour, he felt as if it was too long. "What's on the agenda for the rest of the day?"

Caitlin looked away, pulling her bottom lip between her teeth. "Not a whole lot."

Simon grinned. "Then I have you to myself."

"Not really. I have to leave this afternoon."

"For home?"

"No." She straightened, turning away from him. "I've got to catch a plane in three hours. I'm going to Portland to stay with my sister for a week. She had a baby by Caesarean a couple of weeks ago, and I promised her a long time ago I would come and help her. By the time I'm back you'll be discharged."

"You're leaving," he said flatly.

Caitlin turned to him, but didn't look at him. "I already have the ticket."

"Of course. Of course you have to go. I understand." And he did. He knew the rules. Never let anyone get close, never share anything with someone. He had made them his mantra. And in the past few weeks he had broken each one of them, on his own. If his heart hurt, if he felt a roiling anger beginning, it was his own fault. Well, that was how it went. But now he had one more thing to do.

"Help me sit up," he said shortly.

"But you've been sick."

"I said, help me up, Caitlin."

He could see hurt on her face at the anger in his voice, but he ignored it. He had to start relearning the lessons life had taught him.

She raised the bed slowly and an attack of vertigo gripped him. He rode it out, focusing on the wall above Caitlin's head, forcing himself not to look at her, not to meet her puzzled gaze.

He carefully pivoted himself, swinging his legs over the edge of the bed until he was sitting up without support.

"Simon, what are you doing?" She hurried to his side, her hand automatically catching his shoulder.

"I want to stand up."

"No. You can't."

"The doctor said the plate was fine, didn't he?"

"Yes."

"Well, then. I was standing before I got sick. Help me stand up now." She only stared. "Now," he barked.

She jumped, then he could see her straighten, could almost hear each vertebra snap into place. Now she was angry, as well.

All the better, he thought. It would make everything much easier.

She helped him up and he was surprised to find that his leg didn't hurt nearly as much as it had before. He was healing, just as everyone had promised him.

Caitlin supported him with her arm. His lay across her shoulder. It was just a matter of turning slightly, slipping his other arm around her waist and he had her.

"If you're leaving me, I can't let you go without saying goodbye, can I?" He looked down at her soft green eyes, the delicate line of her cheekbone sweeping down to a narrow jaw. He memorized the curve of her mouth, the faint hollow of her cheeks, each detail of her beautiful, beautiful face. He didn't want to forget her.

She wanted to fight him, he could feel her tense in his arms, but he also knew she didn't dare. Not after what happened the last time. Ignoring the flare of panic in her eyes, he lowered his head, capturing her mouth with his.

She resisted at first, her arms stiffly at her sides, then, as he murmured her name against her lips, as he drew her closer to him, he could feel her soften, feel her arms slip around him, then, hold him close.

His heart tripped, his breath felt trapped in a chest that grew tighter the longer their kiss went on. What he had started in anger, changed with her soft response. When she whispered his name, when her hand reached up to caress his cheek, to hold his head, he felt a melting around his heart and a pain that pierced with a gentle sweetness. Almost he spoke the words, almost he bared his soul.

But he couldn't.

She was leaving and so was he. It wasn't meant to be.

Caitlin sat on the edge of her bed, staring down at the phone in her hand. Jonathon, her brother-in-law had just called her here at Evelyn and Scott's house in Portland. By using his connections in the Royal Canadian Mounted Police, Jonathon had found Jake Steele.

Now Caitlin had the number she had to call and she didn't know if she dared.

It was the best time. The house was quiet. Evelyn and Scott were already in bed, as were the children.

With the time difference, it would only be nine o'clock where Jake lived.

She couldn't stop the restless pounding of her heart, the trembling of her fingers. Was she doing the right thing? Did she have a right to intrude on Simon's life? Simon—who didn't need anyone?

But she thought of her own brother and knew that if something had happened to him, she would want to know. She thought of Simon lying on his hospital bed, staring with longing at Shane's family. She knew in spite of what he had done to her, she had to make this call for him.

Caitlin took another breath, sent up a prayer for wisdom, courage and the right words, and punched in the numbers. The phone rang in her ear, and she felt her heart skip. Another ring. A third.

Disappointment and relief vied for attention. She was going to let it ring one more, no, maybe two more times then she would hang up.

And then what?

Caitlin rubbed her hand over her jeans, waited

and was just about to lower the phone to push the button to end the call when…

"Hello?"

Her heart jumped and she was momentarily speechless.

"Hello?" the voice repeated.

"Hello, Mr. Steele," Caitlin replied breathlessly, frantically searching for the right words. What if Jonathon was wrong? What if this wasn't who he thought it was?

Well, then you make a fool of yourself in front of a stranger you will probably never talk to again, she reassured herself. "My name is Caitlin Severn," she continued struggling to catch her breath. This was ridiculous. She was acting as if she had never made a phone call to a complete stranger before. *A complete stranger who happens to be the brother of a man who you are fascinated and possibly in love with.* "I'm a nurse at Nanaimo General Hospital. I'm calling about a patient I took care of, who I believe is your brother. Simon Steele."

Silence. Utter, heavy and complete silence.

Wrong number, Caitlin thought stifling a hysterical laugh.

"What happened to him?"

Well, it was the right number after all, she thought. "Before you get too concerned," she continued, forcing herself to breathe, to remain calm, "I want to tell you that he's fine now, Mr. Steele. He was in a bad motorcycle accident. Broke his right femur. I was at the accident when it happened and I worked in the ward he was on." She forced herself to stop, to keep from babbling nervously on.

"How do you know he's my brother?"

Because right now, you sound exactly like him, thought Caitlin, hearing the defensive tone enter Jake Steele's voice. This was harder than she thought. "He gave me your first and last name and told me you were his twin. I didn't think there were more than one Jake Steele born on February 16."

"Did he ask you to call me?"

Caitlin bit her lip. "Actually, no."

"Then why are you calling?"

Caitlin fiddled with the edge of her sweatshirt, folding it back and forth as she tried to find the right way to explain her reasoning. From the sounds of things, Jake didn't appear to be any happier to hear about Simon than she presumed Simon would be to hear about his brother.

It disturbed her. "I'm calling because I care for your brother…." The words sounded lame and she knew it. She had been gone from Nanaimo for only four days, and each morning she woke up with a heaviness pressing down on her heart. She had resisted the urge to phone the hospital every day to see how Simon was, reasoning it was better this way. Better for who became less clear each day she was away. She had hoped and prayed that being with her sister and her family would bring clarity to her thoughts. Instead, she felt more confused than before.

She didn't just care for Simon. She loved him.

Caitlin forced her thoughts back to the present, to the phone in her hands and the muted anger of the man on the other end of the line. "Simon sustained very serious injuries and is currently in the hospital in Nanaimo. He's been there for about two weeks. He talked about you and the homes you've been in."

Jake was silent and Caitlin could almost feel the antagonism over the phone. Whatever it was she had expected from this phone call, it wasn't these clipped questions and curt replies.

Somehow she had foolishly thought he would be eager and happy to hear from his long-lost brother. She thought he would be thankful that she took the time to track him down.

"So, why did you think I needed to know this?"

Caitlin straightened, her own anger coming to the fore. "Your brother has been through a lot of pain and has been struggling in many ways, physically as well as spiritually. I called you because in the entire time he was in the hospital, your brother never received one visitor, or one phone call. He is all alone...."

"The fact that my brother doesn't have anyone doesn't surprise me," Jake said, his voice even, almost harsh. "Simon has never needed anyone, never cared for anyone except himself."

Caitlin almost gasped at the coldness of Jake's reply. "I can't believe you're talking like this," Caitlin replied, now thoroughly angry. "He's your brother. Doesn't that relationship mean anything to you?"

"Simon hasn't been a part of my life for a long time now, out of his own choice. If he wants to talk to me I would imagine he could get hold of me."

Caitlin knew the truth of that, but also knew that Simon, for whatever reason, wouldn't do that. "I don't know Simon as well as I would like to," she said, "but I do know that he is seeking and that he is unsure of what he's looking for."

Jake was quiet and Caitlin knew she had touched something in him.

Please Lord, help me find the right words, she prayed as she spoke. "He is your family. I have a brother who I haven't seen for a long time, out of his choice. I know that if something happened to him, I would want to know and I would want to see him again, to be a family again."

"I don't think it's your place to lecture me on family reunions, Miss..." He paused and for a moment Caitlin was tempted to simply hang up and put the Steeles and their brokenness behind her. But she thought of Simon clutching her hand, his eyes full of sorrow and pain he couldn't express and she knew she had to fight for him.

"Severn. Caitlin Severn," she reminded him, clutching the phone, forcing herself to stay calm.

"Well, Miss Severn. I suppose it would be incumbent on me to ask where he is right now."

Incumbent? Oh, brother, Caitlin thought, he sounded just like Charles. *Please Lord, if ever I needed to keep a clear head and a soft tongue it's now. Help me. Help this coldhearted man who I don't even know to understand how important this is.*

"Right now he's in the orthopedic ward of the Nanaimo General Hospital," Caitlin said, forcing her voice to a more even tone. "He's due to be discharged in less than a week, so if you want to see him, I would suggest you go as soon as possible."

"Well, I thank you for your time and persistence, Miss Severn. Unfortunately I'm in the middle of my busiest season. It's been a late harvest and I won't be able to get away for at least another month."

"Please, Jake. I'm not asking for myself. I'm asking for you and Simon. I don't know if you're married...."

"Not currently," he replied curtly and Caitlin sensed there was a whole other story behind those two clipped words, but she kept on.

"Then you and Simon are all each of you have. I would like you to see this as a gift from the Lord. A gift not given lightly." *There was a man all alone.*

He had neither friend nor brother. The words from Ecclesiastes came back to her and in that moment she realized they might just as easily apply to Jake. "I believe that you and Simon are meant to find each other. You're his brother. You can't change that."

Silence again. But Caitlin waited, forcing herself not to try to fill it, to let what she said sink in as she prayed and prayed.

"Like I said, I won't be able to get away for a while, but I will make the effort. I'd like to thank you for your call...."

Which was a neat way of sounding thankful without really being thankful, Caitlin thought. She didn't know if she liked him.

"Are you currently working on the ward?"

"No. I'm staying with my sister in Portland. If you want more information, you can call the hospital. But you are more than welcome to call me, as well." Without waiting for him to ask, she gave him her sister's number as well as the number of the hospital. More silence as she prayed that he wrote them down.

She took a breath and forced herself to continue. "I don't know exactly what happened to you after you and Simon were split," she said. "Simon said that you went to a good home. However, I do know that you and he were raised together in a Christian home. I believe the Lord has brought me to you, and I want you to know that I'll be praying for both of you."

She could almost feel a melting, a relenting coming across the line.

"Thanks," he said, his voice quiet. "And thanks for taking the time to call." Then a *click* sounded in her ear and she knew he had hung up.

Caitlin laid the phone on the bedside table then dropped backward on the bed, her hands trembling, her heart racing. She covered her face with her hands as she prayed.

Please Lord, let Jake go. Let them become brothers again. Reconcile them to each other.

Because it didn't sound as if either of them was too eager to meet again.

"Has Simon Steele been discharged yet?"

Caitlin looked up from her desk with a start at the mention of Simon's name.

"I'm pretty sure this is his coat," the orderly in front of her said, holding up a leather jacket. "It's been hanging around emerg for a while now. One of the nurses who was on duty when he came in just came back from vacation. Said he was up here."

"He was discharged over a week ago. But we can see that it gets to him."

"There were some keys in the pocket and a few other things," the orderly said, handing her a plastic bag holding the personal effects that must have come out of the jacket. "There were a pair of leather chaps, but they got cut to ribbons and had been tossed."

"I'll see that this gets to him," Caitlin said, taking the jacket with a smile.

As the orderly left, Caitlin walked into the office behind the front desk, setting the coat on an empty table. She couldn't stop a foolish trill of her heart at the sight of Simon's coat. She reached out, touching it with a forefinger, tracing the rip in one arm of the coat, the marks left behind when he had gone skidding across the pavement.

She closed her eyes at the memory of him, lying so helpless on the side of the road. His life had been completely rearranged by that one event.

Unfortunately, so had hers.

Caitlin thought her visit to her sister in Portland would have given her back a sense of equilibrium. Instead she'd spent most of her days wondering how Simon was and if Jake had contacted him.

She wondered if he even gave her a second thought. She knew she should forget him, but couldn't. Now, seeing his jacket seemed to bring all the memories she had slowly filed away, flooding back.

She lifted up the bag and, ignoring the voice of caution, opened it up. Inside were a set of keys, as the orderly had said, a folded-up piece of paper, a receipt for a restaurant in Vancouver, and some change. Curious, she unfolded the piece of paper.

But it told her no more about Simon than did the other impersonal effects. It was merely a listing of numbers, some scratched out and a few calculations. On the other side was an address and the name of an apartment block with a phone number underneath it.

Frustrated, Caitlin put the things back in the bag and the bag in the pocket of the coat. It shouldn't matter to her what happened to it, but she knew it did.

"What've you got there?" Eva, one of the other floor nurses walked into the office and laid a folder on the desk.

"It's Simon Steele's jacket," Caitlin said, forcing an impersonal tone in her voice.

"I imagine that will have to get sent back to him."

"Probably." Caitlin shrugged, leaving the room. For a foolish moment she had thought of bringing it back to him herself, of testing the newness of her emotions away from the hospital.

She was crazy she thought, forcing her mind back to her job. But it was difficult. While she was in Portland her sister commented on how listless she seemed.

She *had* been listless and she had tried to pray and reason her way out of it. But ever since Simon had kissed her, she had felt as if her entire world had been flipped end over end. She, who so dearly liked order and control.

Before Charles she had dated precious few men. Too busy getting her degree. Then she wanted to work and then she started dating Charles.

But not even Charles had managed to get her in such a dither, she thought, doodling on the calendar in front of her. She wanted to see Simon again, she didn't want to see him again. All too well she remembered their last time together, the touch of his mouth on hers, his arms around her. She remembered the sorrow in his eyes.

She was sick and tired of her own dithering. In her own lectures to student nurses she talked about patient-nurse intimacy and how it seldom lasted beyond the walls of the hospital. She just didn't know if she wanted to test it out.

Chapter Twelve

"Here's figures on those funds we were talking about before I left on vacation." Oscar dropped a file folder on the desk beside Simon. "I don't know why you're in such a rush on them."

"I want to catch them before they go up," Simon said, clicking on the "save" icon. He leaned back in his chair, wincing as a twinge of pain shot through his leg.

"How's the leg?" Oscar asked sitting down in an office chair beside the desk Simon had set up in one empty corner of his condo.

Oscar had balked at moving their office to Simon's home. Simon had merely stated that it worked easier for both of them. He liked being able to work out of his living quarters. Besides, it gave him another tax write-off. Now he was glad they had done it.

"Some days are better than others."

Oscar shook his head. "I still can't believe you didn't try a little harder to get ahold of me. I would have cut my vacation short, you know that."

"You were camping. How in the world was I supposed to find you."

"The Mounties could have found me."

"It wasn't important." Simon dismissed his comment by grabbing the file folder. "Tell me a little more about these funds."

Oscar's sigh told him Oscar wasn't pleased, but they knew each other well enough to know that he would go along with whatever Simon chose to tell him.

"I've checked out the funds, and it looks like they've bottomed out and should pick up in the next couple of days. European funds are a better bet than Asian these days." Oscar tipped back his chair, his hands locked behind his head.

"Sounds okay. Hear anymore from the contractor on that apartment block in Nanaimo?"

"He gave me a quote. I'm shopping around for a better one yet, but it comes in where it should."

Simon pulled a face. "Don't get too picky. We'll do okay, even with the higher quote."

"We'll do more than okay. The cash flow looks pretty healthy." Oscar glanced around the bare apartment. "I bet we make enough money you could even buy some decent furniture," he said, his tone heavily sarcastic.

Simon looked around and shrugged. "I don't know if I feel like furnishing an apartment. I might sell it."

The condo was large, spacious and sunny. Everything the real estate agent said it would be. But Simon had little inclination to make it a home. It was just like the boat, the trips, all the other toys. Once he had it, it didn't do what he had hoped it would.

He had bought a large leather couch and matching chair at the same time he'd bought the condo. A wall unit stood holding only a stereo and some of the books Simon had collected over the years. He hadn't collected enough possessions over the years to fill such a large space.

Oscar leaned ahead, his elbows resting on his knees. "Would you feel more like fixing up, say—" he hesitated, his hands spreading out "—a Victorian house on five acres, north of Nanaimo, facing the mainland?"

Simon leaned back, making a steeple of his hands. "And why would I want to do that?"

"Because it's a good deal," Oscar held up his hand, ticking off the virtues, "The buyer needs to sell it, and because I think you're ready to buy a house instead of sharing halls and elevators with complete strangers. You need a place to bring a girlfriend."

"I don't know about the last," Simon said, forcing aside thoughts of an angel with soft blond hair and sea-green eyes. Caitlin was out of the question, out of the picture, and he was out of his mind to be even thinking about her. She represented obligations and commitment.

Family.

He got up, pushing aside his own thoughts.

"It's a great deal even from a business standpoint," Oscar continued, leaning back with a creak in the old office chair Simon had bought for his apartment. "And since your accident, I sense you've gone through some soul-searching, some change-of-heart-type stuff. You might even be ready to, dare I say it—" Oscar lowered his voice, his eyes wide, and did a quick drumroll on his knees "—settle down."

"Wishful thinking on your part, Oscar," Simon said shortly. Oscar was too intuitive by half.

"After I met Angela, I would walk around with this dazed look on my face, just like you are now. Someone would be talking to me, and I wouldn't even hear them. Just like you were a few moments ago."

"You won't quit, will you?" Simon said irritably.

"Nope." Oscar rocked back and forth, and Simon resisted the urge to snap at him to sit still.

He was like that more often these days. Irritable and easily angered. Peace eluded him. Before his accident, life had flowed along quite well, but not anymore.

Now all he could think of was Caitlin and the words she had read to him out of the Bible. The passage that offered comfort and at the same time required more of him than he was prepared to give.

All he could think of was how he destroyed the fragile bond building between them with a kiss born out of anger.

A kiss that changed to need and want and a desire to protect and nurture.

"I've got the information you wanted on that company that's going public," Simon said, forcing his mind back to business, back to the safe and predictable. "They're in my bedroom, if you want to get them."

"Okay. Change the subject. I can do this," Oscar said with a laugh, getting up.

The sudden chime of the doorbell broke the quiet.

"Shall I get it?" Oscar asked.

"No. That's okay. The papers are in a folder beside the bed," Simon replied over his shoulder as he walked to the door, wondering who it could be. The home-care nurse stopped by only weekly now and she had come yesterday. He wasn't expecting anyone else to come.

He worked his way slowly across the living room and then to the hallway. This condo was way too big, he thought, trying not to hurry.

Finally he reached the door and opened it.

"Delivery for Simon Steele." A ponytailed delivery boy held out a form for Simon, who signed it. "Do you want me to bring it in for you?" the boy asked, noticing Simon's cane.

"Sure. Just set it on the table there."

Whistling, the boy brought in a package, then sauntered out, closing the door on a very curious Simon.

It was from the Nanaimo General Hospital.

For a weird and wonderful moment he thought it might be something from Caitlin but when he opened it, surprised to see his fingers trembling, he pulled out his jacket.

"What was that?" Oscar walked into the room, frowning at the box on the table.

"My jacket. From the hospital."

"You dropped something." Oscar bent over and picked up a piece of paper, handing it to Simon.

Simon took it, read it and swallowed. It was a note from Caitlin, asking how he was, hoping that all was well with him. Signed with her name. Underneath that, in smaller letters she wrote that she was praying for him.

"What's up, Simon? You look like you've been told your biggest stocks just tanked." Oscar tilted his head, as if to get a better look at his partner. "You okay?"

"Yeah." Simon took a deep breath, rereading the

note as if trying to find something else, some hint of her feelings in it.

"Who's it from?"

"Caitlin," he said without thinking.

"Newest girlfriend?" Oscar asked with a grin. "Is that how she got your coat?"

"No. She works at the hospital. She was my nurse."

"Is she why my tough wheeler-dealer partner is looking as mushy as a cooked marshmallow?"

"Never mind, Oscar," Simon snapped, dropping the letter in the box.

"Ooh. Touchy, too."

"I wasn't mushy."

"Maybe *mushy* was the wrong word. Maybe *wistful* would be better." Oscar sighed dramatically, placing a hand over his heart.

Simon ignored him, putting the coat back on the table. "Can we get back to work?"

"Sure." Oscar grinned as he walked back to the desk. He dropped into a chair. "Caitlin," he said with a tinge of sarcasm and a wink. "I like that name. She's obviously a very organized and caring person. Sending you your coat like that."

"Drop it, Oscar."

Oscar held his partner's gaze, his expression suddenly serious. "I don't know if I will. I've never seen you this flustered, ever. You're cranky on the one hand and on the other, you seem to take things easier. Like I said, I catch you staring off into space. Definitely twitter-pated."

Simon sighed, realizing Oscar wasn't going to let this one go. "Okay. I like Caitlin. You happy now?"

"Nope. Not until I know what you're going to do about it."

"Nothing. Zilch. Nada."

"Which begs the question, why not?"

"Beg all you want. She's off-limits." Simon got up rubbing his leg. It ached again which meant he should probably lie down. But he didn't want to do that, either. "Did you want to go over those funds?"

"No. I want to check out that Victorian house on the Island for you, and I want to see you phone the lady who has you all tied up in knots and ask her out."

Simon sighed, plowing his hand through his hair in frustration. "By all means, check out the house. Maybe you can move there yourself," he said, thoroughly exasperated with his partner.

"Nah. Angela always gets sick on the ferry. You're more flexible than I am, anyhow. Doesn't matter where you live. But I'll check it out for you." Oscar pointed at Simon, winking at him.

"Then do it now. Anything to get you off my back."

"You know, I think I will." Oscar bounded off the couch with a grin and shoved the papers into his briefcase. "Catch ya later, pardner," he said with a smile as he headed out the door.

Simon glared at it as his partner left, feeling pushed and hemmed in by the people in his life. Oscar would never have dared talk to him as he did a few weeks ago. Simon wouldn't have let him.

But as Oscar had said, things had changed. Simon was tired of the loneliness and emptiness of his life. He had allowed Oscar to get closer.

Had allowed Caitlin to get closer still. The downside was the vulnerability, the obligations.

Obligations and the promise of a pair of green eyes that haunted him at every turn.

And the sooner he got that out of his system, the better.

Simon pocketed his car keys, moved the flowers over to his other arm and sighed deeply. A quick glance at his watch showed him that he could figure on the shift change to be happening in about fifteen minutes.

He gave the arrangement a critical once-over. Looked innocuous enough. Carnations and lilies and a few roses.

A very proper thank-you-type bouquet, he figured, no strings attached. It was the least he could do after being such a miserable patient.

He sucked in another deep, cleansing breath, blew it out again, straightened his new leather jacket and then forced himself to move. The December air was chilly, even for the Island, and he hoped the flowers would be protected enough until he got to the hospital.

Once inside, he felt a slight moment of panic. What if Caitlin wasn't working at all?

Well, then, so be it, he thought sauntering down the hallway toward the ward, trying to recapture the laissez-faire attitude that had taken him through other situations with other women. The kind of attitude that gave him a measure of protection.

But his cavalier attitude seemed to dissipate as quickly as frost in the sun when he rounded the corner to the ward and came near the desk. He wiped one palm on his jeans, the other hand still holding the flowers. No one was there.

He looked hopefully around, wondering where everyone was, resisting the urge to just drop off the flowers and go. Then he heard the sound of voices in the room opposite. My old room, he thought, turning.

Danielle walked out laughing. She turned her head and stopped dead in her tracks.

"What are you doing?" Another nurse came up behind her, gave Danielle a light shove and then stopped herself.

"Hi," Simon said, shifting the flowers uselessly to the other hand. He couldn't stop the thrum of his heart at the sight of Caitlin. She wore her hair up today, emphasizing the delicate line of her jaw. Her face was flushed, her eyes bright. She licked her lips once, her hands clasped in front of her and gave him a curt nod.

"Thought I'd drop these off for you ladies," he said, holding up the flowers. "A thank-you for all you did."

Danielle gave Caitlin a nudge, who stepped slowly forward. "Nice to see you again, Simon," Caitlin said softly, taking the flowers. She walked around the desk and set the basket on the ledge, pulling the plastic off. With her eyes still on the flowers, she bent over, sniffing them. "They're beautiful. I'm sure everyone will appreciate them. Thank you."

Her voice was quiet, well modulated, unemotional. Simon wondered if he had done this all wrong.

He shoved his hands in his back pockets and shifted his weight to his good leg. "You're welcome," he said, casting about for something witty and urbane to say. It would have been easy a couple of months ago, but much had happened to him since then.

"How's the leg?" Danielle asked, breaking the silence.

"Good," Simon replied, glancing at her, his eyes returning to Caitlin who still fussed with the flowers. "It hurts once in a while, but even that's getting better."

"And work? How's that going? Still dabbling in the stock market? Got any good tips for some poor lowly nurses? Any inside information?"

Simon forced his attention back to Danielle. "All I can tell you is that helium is up," he said grasping for something, anything that would make Caitlin look up from those infernal flowers and at him.

Caitlin's head came up at his poor attempt at humor, a grin teasing the corner of her mouth. "I suppose diapers remain unchanged," she returned quickly.

Simon felt the tension that held him slowly release and he smiled back at her. "How are you doing, Caitlin?" he asked quietly.

"I think I should get the report ready for the new shift," Danielle said to anyone who cared to listen, then left, leaving Caitlin and Simon looking at each other.

"I'm fine," she said, looking away again. "Been busy on the ward."

"You'll be done in a few minutes?" He asked it as a question even though he knew what the answer would be.

She nodded, glancing sidelong at the clock on the wall. "Ten minutes to be precise."

"You want to go for a cup of coffee?"

She looked up at that, smiling again. "Sure. Sounds good. I have to do a report for the new shift coming on and then I'm done."

"I'll wait for you by the entrance," he said. She nodded her assent and he turned and left, unable to stop his grin.

Pacing around the entrance took up about five minutes. Synchronizing his watch so that it was on time with the clock in the entryway took another sixty seconds. Running his hands over his hair filled fifteen seconds.

Shaking his head at his own behavior, he found an empty chair, picked up a magazine and tried to read about landscaping a summer home. He turned the page to an article about the advantages of shrubs in a backyard.

He thought again about the Victorian that Oscar said he was going to look at. A home. Was he nuts? What did he know about homes and families? Nothing. He had never given himself enough time to figure out how they worked.

Then what are you doing waiting for Caitlin Severn to show up?

He threw the magazine down and instead kept himself busy watching the people, his legs stretched out in front of him, feet crossed at the ankles. You're not proposing to the woman. You're just asking her out for a cup of coffee, he told himself. You've done it hundreds of times before with dozens of other women.

But none of the other women had shown him what Caitlin had shown him. None of them had encouraged him to return to his faith in God, had nurtured a sense of shame and need.

Chapter Thirteen

Caitlin walked down the hall, her steps brisk, efficient. She caught sight of him, then slowed, one hand coming up to smooth her hair.

Simon got up slowly, ignoring the slight pain in his leg.

She wore a yellow anorak and blue jeans. Her hair was loose and at the sight, he smiled. She looked more approachable now. Less a nurse, more a woman.

"Hi," she said, stopping in front of him.

Did he imagine that breathless note in her voice? Was it wishful thinking on his part?

"Hi, yourself." He pulled his car keys out of his pocket, jingling them a minute, just looking at her. "Any place special you want to go to?"

"There's a nice spot past the mall heading up-island," she said, fiddling with her purse straps.

"I've got my car in the parking lot. Do you want a ride with me?"

"Sure."

"Then let's go." They walked in silence out of the hospital, to his car. He unlocked the door for her, watching as Caitlin ducked her head and got in. He walked around the front of the car, his eyes still on her and got in on his side.

He drew in a steady breath as he buckled up and turned the key in the ignition. Caitlin sat back against the headrest, watching him as he backed out of the hospital parking lot and turned onto the road.

"This is a lot different than your motorbike," she said, looking around the interior. "Are you turning over a new leaf?"

"More like starting another book," he said quietly. "The motorbike had to go."

"That sounds profound. How is your leg?"

"Good." Simon drew in a deep breath, smiling. "Really good." He glanced sidelong at her. "And how was your visit with your sister, the one in Portland?"

"Nice. Evelyn and her husband have a lovely little baby girl."

Silence.

Well that exhausted those topics of conversation, he thought.

They drove on for a while, both quiet. Simon never had trouble talking to a woman before, but Caitlin made him uneasy, nervous.

Caitlin glanced at Simon while he gave the waitress their order. His hair was longer than before, hiding the small scar she knew was on his forehead. His eyes held the same glint, his mouth curved up in the same impudent grin. He looked far more at ease than she felt.

His street clothes emphasized his masculinity and at the same time created a distance. This was a Simon unfamiliar to her. Strong, in charge and independent. When she had seen him standing by the desk, she felt as if all the breath had been squeezed out of her chest.

She fiddled with her spoon and, just for something to do, put some sugar in her coffee, stirring it slowly. She could feel Simon's eyes on her but didn't know what to say.

"Isn't this where we are supposed to make intelligent conversation?" he asked suddenly. "You ask me a question, I ask you a question…." He let the comment fade as he smiled at her.

"And the purpose is?"

"Getting to know each other in a neutral setting." Simon set his cup down. "The hospital was definitely your territory. This is just a restaurant. Neutral ground."

Caitlin looked down at her own cup, hardly daring to hope that he wanted the same thing she did. Something had started between them, something she didn't know if she dared explore.

He was right about territory. They had met on the unequal footing of patient and nurse. She had seen his vulnerability. However, he had also voluntarily opened himself up to her in a way no other man had. She had seen him searching for God and that, in itself, touched her deeply.

"I'll start with a question for you, seein's how you're not saying anything," Simon said, pushing his cup and saucer around on the table, a hint of a smile teasing the corner of his mouth. "What new and exciting things have happened in your life? How's the boyfriend?"

Caitlin frowned. "Boyfriend?"

"Yeah. The guy who came to the ward that night. Charles." Simon spun his cup in the saucer, holding her gaze.

"He's not my boyfriend. I broke up with him a while ago."

Simon stopped the spinning, his hand resting on the rim of the cup. "What did you say?"

"I said Charles is not my boyfriend."

Simon sat back, a smile curving his beautiful mouth. "Really."

"I broke up with him the night you had your accident." Caitlin swallowed as she saw the glint in his eyes and knew that in that moment something had shifted, changed. "He came to the ward hoping to get back together with me. I told him again that it was over." She looked down remembering all too vividly the reasons she knew she would never go back to Charles Frost. Remembering Simon's gentle touch and the not-so-gentle kisses of a mouth that now curved up in a smile.

She felt her cheeks warm at the memory and quickly took a sip of coffee to cover up her embarrassment.

"I see," Simon said quietly.

Silence slipped over them as they sat opposite each other. A silence broken by the murmur of the other patrons of the restaurant. She searched desperately for something to say. "And how is your work going?"

Simon lifted a hand and waggled it back and forth. "Good. Making money in some places, losing it in others."

She nodded and that topic was exhausted.

Simon pushed his cup and saucer aside and took her hand in his. "This isn't working really well, is it?" he asked, his deep voice low. "I was hoping we could exchange some idle chitchat, get to know each other better. Start over on a more equal footing." He lifted his eyebrows quickly at that. "If you'll pardon the pun."

Caitlin smiled, her heart thrumming at his contact, her hand nestled in the protective warmth of his. She raised her eyes to his and once again was lost. She had never felt this way about any man before, this sense of belonging, a feeling that with Simon all in her life that was annoying and frustrating became meaningless. "So, how do we do this?"

"I don't know." Simon looked down at her hand, stroking her thumb with his. "I already know that your favorite color is blue, your favorite food is chicken. That you are a great nurse and sincere Christian." He looked up at that, his head tilted to one side. "I know that much about you."

Caitlin swallowed at the intensity of his gaze. "And I know that your favorite color is brown. You like French fries, and you don't like taking painkillers."

His slow, lazy smile wound its way around her heart, tightening it with bands of yearning.

"I know that you have a brother," she continued, striving for an even tone, determined to do this right, to confront all the issues of his life. "That you were raised in foster homes and that deep within you is a need for something more that only God can give. What I don't know is, if you've found it."

"Well, that was quite an exposé," he said, his tone dry.

"It's the truth. And if you want us to get to know each other better, then we had better start on that footing." Caitlin looked down at their joined hands, hoping and praying that she hadn't said too much, yet knowing that she was right.

"Do you want to get to know me better?" Simon asked. Caitlin saw the smirk on his face, but heard in his voice a faint note of yearning, of wanting.

"Yes I do, Simon."

"You might not like what you discover."

"I know what I'm in for," she said quietly.

Now he sat across from her, one hand cradling hers, the other tracing her knuckles. He laughed softly, then looked up at her again. "I don't think you know what you've done to me, Caitlin. For years I've been on my own. I've done what I've wanted to do. I've made money and lost money and none of it mattered. I've never been a responsible kind of guy because I've never wanted to have something that I couldn't afford to lose. But you've made me take another look at myself." He shook his head, as if trying to understand it himself. "I didn't like what I saw. I was angry that you made me vulnerable. I've been trying all my life to be tough and strong. To be independent." He squeezed her hand, hard. "Now I've been reading the Bible, struggling with what God wants me to be. Trying to accept obligations. I don't know if I can do it."

His words alternately warmed and chilled her. "What are you trying to say, Simon?"

Simon lifted her hand up to his mouth and touched his lips to it. "I don't know," he whispered. "I just know that I care about you and that your opinion is important to me." He blew out his breath in a sigh that caressed her hand. "When I was sick, that last night you were with me in the hospital, you were reading that passage from Isaiah, something about comfort. I know what I have to do, but I'm not sure

I'm ready to do it yet." He shrugged and gently lowered her hand to the table.

Caitlin smiled. "Well, then I guess I have to keep praying for you, Simon."

He smiled back and gave her hand a quick squeeze. "You do that, Caitlin Severn."

The talk had gotten heavy, yet Caitlin felt a lightness pervade the atmosphere. As if a foundation had been laid. But she could see from Simon's frown that it was time to change the subject.

"So, tell me about Oscar. How in the world did you two ever meet up?"

Simon lifted his head smiling. "That's a long story."

Caitlin shrugged, glancing at her watch. "I've got tomorrow off, so I've got time."

So he told her. The talk moved from Oscar to books they had read, places they'd been. Simon was well traveled, she discovered. He'd been to places she had only dreamed of seeing, done things she had only imagined. Scuba diving off the Tasmanian coast, trekking in Nepal, taking his chances on the Trans-Siberian railway. She shook her head with every new adventure.

"My life sounds horribly dull," she said after he'd recounted a harrowing trip on a bus through Africa.

Simon shrugged her comment away. "Traveling can be dull, too. Planes and hotels and rented cars. It's all the same after a while, if you're on your own."

He caught her eye and smiled a lazy smile. "It's more fun with someone."

Caitlin's breath caught in her throat at the suggestion in his eyes, his smile.

"Aren't there places you would love to go, Caitlin?" he asked, his voice lowering almost intimately.

"Lots. I've always wanted to see Paris and Greece. The usual tourist travel destinations. I'm not much for adventure, I guess."

"I liked Paris. But it's not a city you should visit on your own," Simon said, leaning slightly forward, one corner of his mouth curved up in a smile. "Paris needs to be seen walking arm in arm with someone you care about." He took her hand again, playing with her fingers.

Caitlin felt her breath catch in her throat, felt her heart slow, miss a beat, then race as she understood the suggestion in his voice, his posture.

What am I going to do with this man, Lord? He confuses me, makes me afraid, makes me want to care for him. She swallowed, her hand still in his as he ran his index finger over hers again and again.

He looked up at her, his eyes intent, and Caitlin knew that if the table hadn't separated them, he would have kissed her.

And she would have let him.

The drive to Caitlin's home was done in silence, an awareness humming between them. Each time

Simon glanced sidelong at Caitlin, he could see her eyes glowing in the reflected light of his car's dashboard.

He couldn't suppress the feelings of unworthiness that her gentle smile gave him. But he also knew that in spite of his feelings, he had to see her again. It was like a hollow need that only she could fill. He didn't like the hold she had over him, but he liked even less the notion of not seeing her again.

They pulled up to her house, the front window shedding light in the gathering darkness.

"Thanks for the ride," she said, reaching for the door handle. "And the coffee."

Simon watched her turn, watched as she pulled her purse close to her in readiness to get out. "Wait" he said softly, catching her arm.

She turned to face him, her eyes wide. "What?"

Simon let his eyes drift over her face, come to rest on her softly parted mouth. Ignoring the cold voice of reason, he bent over and fitted his mouth to hers. The kiss started out so gentle, so plain, but then she murmured his name, slipped her arms around him, pulled him closer.

And he was undone. He caught her close, almost crushing her, his mouth slanting over hers.

Simon was the first to draw away, his eyes seeking hers, his hand reaching up to touch her mouth in wonder.

"What are you doing to me?" he murmured, remembering his own response the last time he had kissed her. The absolute rightness of having her in his arms, the sweetness that pierced him when she spoke his name.

"Kissing you, I thought," she replied, her voice trembling.

Simon drew in a careful breath, unable to suppress the smile that threatened to crack his jaw. He stroked her hair back from her face, just because he wanted to. He didn't want to think about what was happening to him, didn't want to think that he was running the risk of making himself vulnerable to another person. This was Caitlin. She wasn't just anybody, he reasoned.

"Are you busy tomorrow?" he asked, looking down into her soft green eyes, losing himself in their warmth.

She shook her head. "Not until the evening," she whispered.

"How would you like to take a trip up-island? I have a place I want to have a look at." Not the most romantic date he had ever taken a woman on, but he sensed with Caitlin he needed to take things slow. For his own protection as much as anything. Maybe spending some more time with her would ease the ache thinking about her created in him.

Maybe pigs could fly, he thought.

"I'd like that," she said with a soft murmur. She touched his cheek, stroking it lightly with warm fingers.

"Good," he replied turning his head to kiss her fingertips. "I'll pick you up at three."

She traced his mouth, smiling up at him. "Then I'll see you tomorrow," she said, leaning closer to press a light kiss on his lips.

Then she opened the car door, letting a blast of cold air in, jumped out and was striding up the walk to her parents' house before he had a chance to open his own door.

He got out and called to her over the hood. "You're supposed to let me walk you to the door."

She turned, walking backward, laughing at him. "Next time," she said. Then tossing a wave at him, she turned and jogged up the steps and went into the house.

Bemused, Simon got back in his car, put it in gear and drove away. He felt bamboozled by what had happened. He had gone to the hospital simply to deliver flowers and ended up with a date with Caitlin Severn tomorrow. He wondered if he knew what he was getting himself into.

Chapter Fourteen

"What do you plan to do with it?" Caitlin asked, as Simon unlocked the front door of the old Victorian house.

"It's an investment," Simon replied, standing aside to allow Caitlin to walk into the main foyer. Their footsteps echoed in the large open hallway. To one side was a set of doors, now boarded up. The other set of doors led to a large open room and a hallway flanked the large, wide stairs directly in front of them.

"Oh, look at that." Caitlin ran up the first flight of stairs, stopping at the landing. A stained-glass window shed a colored pattern of diffused light on the landing. "This doesn't look Victorian."

"I suspect one of the hippies that lived here made it." Simon came up beside her, his hands in his pockets.

They walked upstairs, inspecting each room. The heavy odor of incense hung in one of the rooms and in the other, dark paper covered a broken window. Water stains on the ceilings attested to the need for a new roof.

"It's going to be a pile of work, Simon. Are you sure you want to even bother?" Caitlin shook her head as they walked down the hall.

Simon shrugged, reaching around her to open the door of the last room. "A person could always bulldoze it and build a new one." He had to push to open the door and when they stepped inside the room, Caitlin had to stop her surprised gasp. Windows from floor to ceiling ran along one wall and flowed in a three-quarter circle instead of a corner to the other wall. "This is beautiful," she breathed, walking farther into the room, straight to the semicircle of windows. "Wouldn't a set of chairs be just perfect here?" She stepped closer to the window, resting her fingertips lightly against it as if to touch the view.

Beyond the shoreline below them, beyond the water, she could see the mountains of the mainland with their variegated colors of blue, mauve and grey. A few gulls wheeled past them, celebrating their utter freedom punctuated by their piercing cries.

"This is just incredible." She glanced over her shoulder, disconcerted to see Simon directly behind her. His hands were safely in the pockets of his khaki pants, holding back his leather jacket, but the way he looked down at her left her with no illusions as to what was on his mind.

"It is incredible," he agreed, his hazel eyes twinkling down at her.

"I meant the view, Simon," she said breathlessly.

His lazy smile crawled across his beautiful mouth. "So did I," he replied.

Caitlin looked away, fully aware of Simon behind her, aware of the fact they stood in what was probably the master bedroom of this large, rambling house. For a brief moment she allowed herself a fantasy. Simon and her, standing together, looking out over a view they saw day after day.

It would be early morning. They would each be getting ready for work, but taking time to just be together, sharing a quiet moment before the busyness of the day separated them.

She let her eyes close as she hugged herself, unaware of the fact that she was slowly leaning back toward Simon until barely a breath separated them. Then his arms surrounded her, held her against him, his face buried in the hair that lay on her neck.

"Caitlin," he breathed, holding her closer, rocking her slightly.

It was a small movement, a mere twisting of her head, a shifting of her weight, and her cheek touched his forehead. He lifted his head and once again, their lips met in a kiss as soft as a baby's sigh.

He was the first to draw back, and Caitlin murmured her disappointment. He dropped a light kiss on her forehead and then stepped back.

Caitlin felt bereft and frustrated at the same time. She knew something important was building between them, but at the same time she didn't know if she should trust her own feelings. She cared for Simon deeply and if she were to truly examine her feelings, she would be able to say she loved him.

But she didn't dare say so, and so far he hadn't expressed how he truly felt about her. Once before she had made a mistake and wasn't eager to spend another few years of her life wondering about another relationship.

If she were to face the truth, she would realize that she was afraid to push Simon too hard. She knew enough about his life to know that Simon was afraid to tie himself down. Buying this house could be a signal that he was ready to do so, but then again, Simon was a consummate businessman. It could just be another investment.

Caitlin turned back to the view, frustrated with herself, frustrated with emotions she couldn't control. *Please Lord,* she prayed, wrapping her arms around herself, *show me what I should do. I'm confused. I'm afraid I love him, and I'm afraid that love will go nowhere. Help me to trust You, help me to be satisfied with Your love first and foremost.*

"We should be getting back."

Simon's voice broke into her prayer, and she turned to face him, forcing a smile to her face. He only stared at her, his own expression slightly dazed. Then he abruptly turned around, the sound of his booted heels echoing in the silence of the house.

Caitlin followed him more slowly, glancing over her shoulder once more at the remarkable room with the wonderful windowed nook.

Then she relegated her own wisp of a daydream back where it belonged. Reality.

"So, what's the verdict?" Simon asked as they drove away from the property.

Caitlin craned her neck for one last look then turned to Simon. "I think you should buy it. If nothing else, you could turn it into a bed-and-breakfast."

Simon pursed his lips, nodding at her suggestion. "Could do that." He glanced sidelong at her, then quickly away again. "I'd have to find someone to run it for me, though."

Their conversation seemed to carefully pick its way through dangerous territory, Caitlin thought. Simon hardly dared say that he might want the house for himself and she didn't dare suggest it. To do so would give a wrong signal, create a misunderstanding.

How she hated this stage of the relationship, she thought. She had gone through it enough times with Charles, she should be good at it. The hesitation, the uncertainty. Wondering if you were presuming too much. Wondering if it was going to go beyond a few kisses, a few casual dates.

In spite of all the gains women said they had made in terms of equality over the past few years, they hadn't made many strides when it came to women being able to read men, or vice versa.

He pulled up in front of her house and Caitlin turned to him, deciding to stick her neck out a bit. "Would you like to come in? It's my mother's birthday party."

Simon shrugged, biting his lip as he looked past her to the house.

"I can't intrude on that."

"You don't intrude on families, Simon," she said quietly. "Just come in for a quick cup of coffee. Say hi to my parents, wish my mom a happy birthday."

Simon blew out his breath in a sigh, still contemplating.

Please, Lord, let him say yes, she thought. She wanted him in her home. She wanted him to meet her family. In some foolish way she felt it would show her whether she was wasting her time or not.

She didn't want to feel that way about Simon because in spite of her doubts, she knew she was falling in love with him.

"Okay," he said quietly, giving her a quick grin. "I'll do that."

Caitlin let out her breath, not even aware she was holding it. Then with a grin she couldn't suppress, she got out of the car, waiting for him to catch up to her and together they walked up the path to her home.

As soon as they opened the door, Caitlin wondered if she had made a grave mistake. She heard the unmistakeable tones of Rachel's laughing voice, Jonathon's deep one and those of her grandparents.

"Got extra company," she said with forced brightness as they walked in the door. Caitlin took his coat and hung it up in the cupboard in the entrance. Then taking a breath for courage, walked through the arched entryway into the living room.

"Oh, hi, Caity," her mother said from the couch directly facing the opening. "I'm so glad you made it back. I…"

But whatever she was about to say died on her lips when she saw Simon. She glanced back at Caitlin with a puzzled look, then back at Simon.

Caitlin almost groaned. She just knew her mother was mentally comparing Simon to Charles.

"Everybody," she said encompassing the entire room with a casual wave of her hand, forcing an overly bright smile. "I'd like you to meet Simon."

The introductions were made. Simon was gracious. He wished Caitlin's mother a happy birthday. He was witty and made Rachel laugh. Rachel tossed Caitlin a bemused look but thankfully was politeness personified when introduced.

Caitlin kissed her grandparents and listened to her

grandfather's usual doctor joke. Grandma gave her a kiss and asked when she was coming over again. Her mother couldn't hide her surprise. Thankfully her father covered up by clearing the newspapers off a love seat, indicating they should sit there.

A moment of silence followed as Caitlin and Simon sat down, then...

"Do you want some birthday cake and coffee?" her mother offered both of them.

"How is work going?" Rachel asked Caitlin, with a knowing smirk.

"So what do you do?" Jonathon asked Simon at the same time.

"Where did that dog go now?" her father muttered to no one in particular.

The dog was retrieved from under the couch and sent downstairs to sulk. Her mother left to get Simon and Caitlin each a cup of coffee but not before she threw Caitlin a slightly puzzled look.

Soon the usual ebb and flow of family conversation filled the room again as Caitlin answered the "duty" questions about her work from her grandparents and asked after Rachel's health. From that the topics ranged from the traffic coming off the ferry to politics to the best way to get rid of fleas on dogs. Caitlin laughed with her sister, answered her grandparents' frequent questions and occasionally glanced sideways at Simon. He was talking to Jonathon, but would, from time to time, look at her. His expression was unreadable, and Caitlin felt a stirring of disquiet. When he smiled it was forced. As he sat drinking his coffee, he sat on the edge of the couch, as if ready to bolt.

Simon finally finished his coffee, set down the cup and then stood up. "Mr. and Mrs. Severn, it was nice to meet you and best wishes again on your birthday," he said, his voice achingly polite. He said his fare-wells to the rest of the family and with a quick look at Caitlin left.

She followed him, her discomfort growing.

"What's wrong, Simon?" she asked as he pulled his jacket off the hanger in the entrance. He glanced over her shoulder at the group who she knew was watching them. She lowered her voice. "Did some-one say something wrong?"

He snapped up his coat, the sounds echoing in the quiet. "Come say goodbye to me outside," he said, turning to open the door.

Caitlin hugged herself against a sudden chill as they stepped outside, closing the door quietly behind her. "What's the matter?"

He shoved his hands in his coat pocket, the over-head porch light casting his face in shadows. She couldn't read his expression, couldn't understand what precisely was happening, but her inner sense told her it wasn't good.

"Nothing's the matter. Your family didn't say any-thing wrong. They seem like wonderful people."

She relaxed at that, her shoulders losing their tension. "I'm glad you like them."

"I do. You're a lucky woman, Caitlin." She could see his careful smile. "No, not lucky. Blessed." He leaned closer and touched his lips to hers. A brief kiss, gentle and soft.

Then he turned and sauntered down the walk to his car, got in and drove away.

Caitlin watched his rear lights until he turned, then she leaned back against the door.

He had denied it, but she knew, deep inside, something had happened. Something very wrong.

It had been seventeen days, Caitlin figured, glancing at the calendar hanging on the wall in her parents' kitchen. Seventeen days since Simon had walked away from her standing on her parents' porch.

And he hadn't called.

How could she have been so stupid? she thought. Simon had dangled her along from the first time she met him. Back and forth, back and forth. Like she was some kind of fish on a hook. A kiss here and there, a serious conversation and then he pulled back again.

A sucker, she thought angrily, pushing her chair back and getting up, that's what she was. First Charles, now Simon. It seemed it was her fate to end up with guys who were afraid to commit.

She glanced at her watch. In an hour Danielle was

going to pick her up to go Christmas shopping. And she dreaded it.

The season had sneaked up on her, she thought with a rueful shake of her head. Usually she was in the thick of preparations, helping her mother bake and putting up decorations long before it was time.

But not this year. This year it was a chore, a burden to get even the most simple of tasks done. The Christmas spirit was decidedly missing in her life.

And she knew exactly why.

She had prayed, had read her Bible, had talked to her sisters, but she couldn't seem to get around the problem of her love for Simon. Because much as she didn't like to face it, she did love him.

She wasn't able to analyze exactly why. He was exasperating, complicated, troubled.

But each time she thought of him, it was with a trembling heart and a yearning to be with him again. He made her complete, whole.

She wandered around the house, from the kitchen to the living room. A Christmas tree sat in one corner, a few presents under it already. Her mother had made up arrangements of cedar and candles and laid boughs of cedar on the mantel of the fireplace. Clusters of cedar bound with bright red ribbon hung on the wall bracketing an embroidered nativity scene her mother had done years ago.

The aroma of cedar and fir filled the house.

Her sisters were on the phone every other day, making plans, gearing up for another Severn family get-together. Tony had even called, much to her parents' delight and surprise.

Caitlin wondered if anything had ever come of her phone call to Simon's brother.

And then she thought of Simon. Again.

She was tired of feeling this confused and frustrated. She walked back to the kitchen and taking a steadying breath, sat down by the phone. She knew his number by heart. Sad, really.

It rang once, then again and she wondered if he was on the road, wheeling and dealing again.

On the fourth ring, someone picked up.

Even over the sterile medium of the phone line, his deep voice could give her shivers, she thought fatuously.

"Hello, Simon. Caitlin here."

Silence hung heavy over the line.

"Hello, Caitlin."

She wished she could see his face, wished she could see his expression. But all she had to go on was his voice. And that didn't sound too welcoming.

She decided to forge ahead. "I hadn't heard from you in a while," she said. "You must be busy," she added hopefully.

"Yeah." Silence again.

"I was wondering if that was the reason I haven't heard from you."

"Well things have been hectic with that new apartment block."

"What about the house?"

"I've decided to give it a miss. Didn't seem like a good investment."

"I see." And she did. Silly as it sounded, the house seemed to represent settling down, a desire on his part for more than a sterile apartment. Her silly fantasy had been just that. She would have gladly shared that home with him. But Simon only saw opportunities.

"Look, Caitlin. I've got to go. Oscar is coming pretty soon...."

"Am I going to see you again?"

A hesitation, then Simon cleared his throat. "Caitlin, I'm sorry." He paused and in that moment Caitlin felt her throat thickening, choking her. She swallowed and swallowed, afraid of the next words, willing them out of him, yet at the same time wanting to slam the phone on the hook so she wouldn't hear them.

"Caitlin, it just isn't going to work between us," he continued.

"Explain that please," she said abruptly. How could he say that? They had shared so much. She remembered reading Isaiah to him, talking to him, sharing. She felt more complete with him than she had with Charles, with any man she had met.

"You're a great person and you've got a lot going for you…."

"Spare me the platitudes, just give me the truth." She forced the words out, clutching the phone so hard she was surprised it was still intact.

"I have nothing to give you Caitlin."

She forced a laugh. "Whatever do you mean, Simon? I thought you had quite a bit of money."

"I know money isn't important to you, Caitlin. But I know family is. And I can't give you that." He paused. "I'm sorry."

"Don't you dare hang up yet, you coward," she blurted, hardly believing she actually spoke the words out loud. "I don't know where you come off thinking that family is like a dowry, an endowment you bring to a relationship. I know where you come from. I know where you've been…."

"No, you don't Caitlin." Simon's voice was hard now. "You don't know and don't presume to think you do."

"Do I need to experience precisely the same thing to be able to understand you?" She got up, pacing back and forth, trying to find some outlet for her anger, her frustration. "I have agonized over our relationship. I have wondered what I really feel for you. I've lain awake nights over you, I've watched over you. I've prayed for you and loved you. And now you so casually tell me 'it won't work' just because I have a family and you don't. I've been told by one ex-boyfriend that 'it won't work' because I don't want to move, but never because I happen to come from a loving home."

"You really don't understand do you?" he growled. "It's over, Caitlin." He hesitated while Caitlin drew in another breath to give him another blast. "It's over." Then unbelievably, she heard a click of the phone in her ear. She looked at it, dumbfounded, then slowly hung up.

She turned around, walked upstairs to her bedroom, sank down on her bed. Then she buried her face in her hands and wept.

She cried for herself, for Simon and his confusion and for the pain she heard in his voice. She cried for all the brokenness in this cold lonely world that created people without families, without a parent's love.

When the worst of her heartache had flowed over her and dissipated, she lay back on the bed, her eyes sore from the sorrow, staring sightlessly up at the ceiling. In spite of her own sorrow, she couldn't help her prayer. *Please be with Simon,* she whispered. *Please show Him Your love and Your comfort. Help me to understand. Show me what to do.* Somehow, she knew she and Simon weren't finished yet.

Simon laid the phone down and pressed his fingers against his eyes. He sucked in a deep breath.

"I've prayed for you, loved you."

Caitlin's words were spoken in anger, but he heard the absolute sincerity behind them.

He knew he had done the right thing by breaking up with her. He knew any relationship with Caitlin would go beyond casual. All the way to marriage and what kind of father would he be? What did he know of parenting, of how families worked? He came from nowhere and had nothing.

Sitting in Caitlin's house with her family had reminded Simon far too vividly of each time he was moved into a new home. Those first few weeks of uncertainty, of trying to figure out how this family worked, of wondering if this was going to be a good home or bad home. The feeling of not belonging, of being on the outside of a family that had been together long before him and would still be together after he left.

He had spent half his life outrunning responsibilities, the ties that a family like Caitlin's entailed would bind around him. He hadn't given himself time to maintain close friendships, hadn't bothered to get to know anyone other than Oscar on the most casual basis.

Somewhere in Alberta he had a brother he hadn't talked to in so long, he wouldn't even know how to begin reestablishing their long-lost relationship. There was no forgiveness for that long a silence and he knew it.

The end result of all that was he had nothing to give Caitlin.

"I've prayed for you, loved you."

Her words echoed through his mind. Blowing out a sigh, he dragged his hands over his face then looked up.

He needed to get some work done, that's what. He never spent this much time contemplating his own life before. Never gave himself enough time to do it.

He flipped on the computer and as he waited for it to boot up, picked up the estimate a contractor had sent him on renovating the apartment block in Nanaimo. Under the file folder lay a Bible.

Simon glanced at it.

He remembered a quiet voice reading to him through the delirium of his fever. *Comfort, comfort ye my people.* Words that soothed, filled, smoothed the rough places of his life. Caitlin had stayed at his side then, as well.

Simon didn't deserve her, he knew that. But he also knew that he couldn't put her out of his mind. It was sheer cowardice on his part that kept him away from her. He hadn't been able to run, but he had retreated.

But oh, how he had missed her. He knew he cared for her more deeply than he had for anyone. He knew that every time he thought of her, his heart ached. Love shouldn't hurt, he thought. Love was supposed to be a soft, gentle emotion, not these hooks that dug into his heart.

Frustrated with his own thoughts, he picked up the Bible, leaned back in his chair, crossed his legs at the ankle and started leafing through it.

He turned to Isaiah 40. "Comfort, comfort my people, says your God." Caitlin had certainly followed that command, he thought with a sad smile. He read on until he came to Isaiah 41. "I took you from the ends of the earth, from its farthest corners I called you. I said, 'You are my servant;' I have chosen you and have not rejected you. So do not fear, for I am with you; do not be dismayed, for I am your God. I will strengthen you and help you; I will uphold you with my righteous right hand."

He laid his head on the high back of his computer chair, letting the words become a part of him. *Called, chosen.* Not *rejected.*

He had been here before, he thought. In the hospital. That last night he had been with Caitlin. He remembered his broken dreams. Words and snatches came back to him now. *My son, give me your heart,* he remembered.

He had hesitated then. To give one's heart was to open oneself up to weakness, to give someone something to hold over you.

But what was the alternative, he thought, opening his eyes and looking around his stark apartment. Keeping to yourself, making more money? Eating your heart out over a beautiful woman with a gentle smile?

His life seemed rather pathetic right now. Empty and purposeless. He closed his eyes. The Bible was still open on his lap. He knew what he had to do. He just wasn't sure exactly how to go about it. *Show me, Lord. Help me through this,* he prayed. *I can't go on like this. I love her. I know I do. I know what You want of me. I don't like being weak. I don't like letting others be in charge, but I'm hereby putting You in charge of my life.* He stopped, as if analyzing the data, then shook his head. *I'm letting go. I surrender.*

And at that moment, as he mentally pried his fingers from all the events of his life that he clung to so tightly, he felt a lightness, a peace pervade him.

He spent the next half hour paging through the Bible, remembering passages that Tom Steele used to read. He reacquainted himself with a book that had once been a part of every meal, every evening before bed.

And he slowly felt the tension leave his shoulders. He laid the Bible aside with a rueful grin. Salvation or no, he still had some work to do. And he still had to figure out how he was going to reconcile himself with Caitlin, praying he hadn't blown it.

The harsh peal of the doorbell broke his concentration on the computer. With a dazed glance he looked up. Darkness had fallen while he had worked.

He wondered who it could be. For a brief moment the thought pierced him that it might be Caitlin. But common sense told him to forget that idea.

Simon got up, walked to the door, opened it and frowned.

A tall figure stood backlit by the light from the hallway. He wore a red plaid jacket over a denim shirt tucked into denim jeans. Cowboy boots completed the picture.

"Simon Steele?" the man asked.

Simon nodded, then, as the voice filtered through his memories he felt the blood drain from his face, felt his heart slow.

"Jake?"

Chapter Fifteen

"Hello, Simon," Jake replied, his hands hanging at his sides, not making a move in his brother's direction.

Simon couldn't help but stare. It was Jake all right. Same dark hair with a tendency to wave, same brown eyes that looked steadily at the world from beneath level brows. Same uncompromising mouth. Same Jake, only older.

Simon forced his gaze away. "Come in," he said, stepping aside, shock making him almost incoherent.

He flicked on some lights as Jake walked into the room.

Jake stopped halfway, not sitting down, just looking at his brother. But what do you say after all those quiet years? Their last phone call had been full of anger and accusations and they hadn't spoken to each other since.

Now two grown men stared across the room at each other as the silence stretched out.

Finally Simon asked, "How did you find me?"

Jake sat down then, his elbows resting on his knees. "I got a phone call," he said slowly, clasping his hands. "From a woman named Caitlin. She called when you were still in the hospital. I would have come to visit you then, but she called in the middle of fieldwork. We were way behind so I couldn't come."

Simon sat down at that. Caitlin again. Dear, sweet, wonderful, beautiful, organizing Caitlin. "How did she find you?"

Jake lifted one shoulder, shaking his head. "Don't have a clue." He looked up at Simon. "I thought you might have told her."

"I haven't talked to you in over twelve years." Simon blew out his breath as the reality of the words settled in for both of them. He looked at his brother as he struggled to find something that would bridge the gap of time and space between him and one of the few people in his life that he had ever truly loved.

Jake looked up and for a moment their eyes held. Jake was the first to look down, pressing his thumbs together and apart. "So, what kind of work have you been doing these past years?"

Chitchat, thought Simon. A warming up, a way of circling and checking each other out from the safe distance of work and occupation. "I own a few franchises, dabble in stocks and bonds." Simon laughed shortly as he heard his job through his brother's ears. "What about you?"

Jake pursed his lips, tilted his head to one side. "I'm farming with Fred Prins. My foster father."

"So you stayed there?"

Jake nodded. "I was fortunate there."

Simon clasped his hands over his stomach, letting a silence drift up between them, full of memories. "So, you ever get married?" he asked finally.

Jake laughed shortly. "Yes. I have a little girl. My wife is dead, though."

Simon sensed a history there, but didn't pursue it, recognizing the need to keep things light for now. "Well I didn't. Always been restless, I guess."

More silence. They both knew what the end result of that restlessness had been.

"So, how long can you stay?" Simon asked.

"I've got a couple of days off. I thought I would stay around for a while tomorrow. I have to be back the next day, though. Christmas is coming."

Simon nodded, feeling a clutch of sorrow at the mention of Christmas. He was usually gone this time of the year. However, for now his sorrow was alleviated by the reality of his brother, here. A brother who wanted to reconnect the broken thread of their mutual past. Family.

"Did you have supper?" Simon asked.

"I grabbed a burger at Blue River," Jake said.

"Then you're probably ready for something else. We could go out, but you're probably tired. I'll order in."

Half an hour later they sat across from each other at the table—a steaming pizza in a box between them. Bachelor food, thought Simon wryly. Jake paused a moment, bowing his head, and Simon realized he was asking a blessing.

Simon did the same. *I'm a little rusty at this, God,* he prayed, *I'm not exactly sure what I should be saying, but thanks.* He paused then added, *Thanks for Jake.* He lifted his head and caught Jake's surprised look. He ignored it and started eating. When they were done, they moved to the living room, settling into an awkward silence.

"Why don't you ask me the questions you want to, Jake," Simon said after a few minutes, knowing he wanted to get things out in the open. "We can get all of this stuff from our past out of the way."

"We'll never get it *all* out of the way," Jake said, standing up and turning to face his brother. "Things don't just go away because you've decided they will."

Simon held his brother's steady gaze. "You came a long way to see me, Jake. I think you're allowed a few questions."

"Okay." Jake plowed his hand through his hair, rearranging the neat waves. "May as well get to it. Did you ever find Mom?"

"No. I would have called you if I did."

"Would you have?" Jake asked, his short laugh sounding harsh. "It would have been nice if you had, anyhow. Because I didn't have the first clue where you were, Simon. In over ten years not a letter, a phone call, not even a postcard or a message sent via someone else. I thought you were dead, man. I really thought you were dead."

And as Simon listened to the pain in his brother's voice, he was forced to face the consequences of his own actions.

"I remember asking why you always ran, and you'd say you were looking for Mom. Were you really?" Jake's voice was quiet now.

Simon shrugged. "At first I was. After Dad Steele died, I hated the idea that we got moved and had no say. I missed Dad and I didn't know how to show it. So I would take off."

"The social workers would get so ticked off at you for running away all the time. I remember how flustered our foster parents would get," Jake said.

"The one, Mary Arnold, would always cry and her husband would yell."

"I think they liked us but couldn't handle the stress. So we got moved again."

"For what it's worth, Jake, I'm sorry," Simon said quietly.

"Well, we only went through one more. Then we were split up…."

"And you landed on your feet at the Prins's home," Simon said wistfully. "I was always jealous of you, you know that?"

"You didn't like it at your last foster home, did you?"

Simon shook his head. "The Stinsons were decent people but hard. I used to hate it when she would punish me by taking away visits with you." Simon smiled. "I always enjoyed our visits together. I remember coming to visit you at the Prins's, and Mrs. Prins would always give me a big hug. It was about the only time I got one."

"Really?"

Simon held his brother's gaze. "Yeah, Jake. Really."

"You never said."

"C'mon. We were fifteen. What guy of that age is going to admit that he still likes to get a hug?" Simon shrugged off the memory. "Like I said, the Stinsons did what they were supposed to, but I didn't get a lot of affection there."

"That why you ran away?"

"Partly. I was sick of getting told what to do. I was a cocky, mixed-up sixteen-year-old who had some weird notion of finding our mother so that you and I could get back together again. You were so happy at the Prins's home, I knew you wouldn't run away unless I gave you a good reason to."

"Tilly and Fred Prins treated me like a son. Running away to find our mother was a dead end."

"I didn't look that hard, Jake," Simon conceded. "I didn't have the time, money or resources. And after a while, I didn't even have much of a reason."

"Do you think we might find her yet?"

"I'd like to think we might."

"If we both put our energy behind it, we could find out if she's still alive or not."

Simon had always lived under the impression that Jake wasn't interested in looking into their past. "Sounds good to me. I'd like to connect with her, be a family again. When I was in the hospital, the kid next to me would get visits from his family. And I would get jealous…."

"If I had known…"

"Doesn't matter Jake. You're here now and for that I thank God."

They spent the rest of the evening catching up, exchanging idle chitchat, reconnecting.

The next morning Simon and Jake went to a restaurant for breakfast and Jake asked him who Caitlin was.

"A nurse at the hospital."

"But she didn't call from the hospital."

"No?" Simon was surprised. "Where did she call from?"

"Said it was her sister's place. She seems like a great person, Simon," Jake continued. "When she phoned I wasn't exactly hospitable, but she kept at me."

"She does that well," conceded Simon with a wry grin.

"She told me that she believed God had brought her to me and told me she would be praying for us."

He laughed lightly, pouring syrup over his pancakes. "Told me that you and I needed to be a family again."

"Family's pretty important to her. As is her faith." Simon fiddled with his eggs.

"I get the feeling that she's special?"

Special? The word was totally inadequate to describe the hunger that clutched him when he thought of her. The regret that he felt just now. "I think I love her, Jake," he said, unable to keep the words down, needing to talk to someone about it. Who better than his own brother?

"That's great."

Simon sighed. "I guess."

"So, what's the problem?" Jake continued.

"She's a wonderful person, just like you guessed. Her faith is so strong and so much a part of her," Simon continued, staring into the middle distance, thinking about her. "She comes from a secure, happy family. I don't know if I can give her the same. I've run away from every family I've been a part of."

"Don't underestimate what you have to offer." Jake forked up a piece of pancake. "She must care for you. Why else would she call?"

Simon hardly dared believe what his brother said. He knew he and Caitlin shared something. He knew that he loved her dearly. But for the rest of their time together, Caitlin wasn't mentioned again.

They walked back to Simon's apartment, talking, catching up. "You want to come to the farm for Christmas?" Jake asked after a moment. "I know you'll be more than welcome."

Simon shrugged, his hands in his pockets, his shoulders hunched against the cold. "I don't know. I usually spend Christmas in warmer places. I wouldn't know what to do."

"What's to do? You show up, eat, laugh. Come to church. You could meet my little girl."

Simon smiled as he opened the door of his condo for his brother. "A niece. Imagine that."

"She's a cutie 'Uncle Simon'." Jake nudged him. "You'd love her."

"Uncle Simon. That has a nice ring to it." Simon tried to imagine Jake with a little girl, tried to see himself as an uncle. Family.

"So are you going to come?"

Simon pulled in a deep breath and blew it out again. He had missed Caitlin more each day, wanted to be with her. *I've loved you, prayed for you.* Her words haunted him. He had told her it was over, yet he knew he would never forget her.

"No," he said suddenly, shrugging off his coat. "I think I should finish off some unfinished business first."

"Caitlin?"

Simon caught his lip between his teeth and nodded.

"I think that's wise. She sounds like a sincere, warm person. I didn't come across real well when I talked to her, but she didn't hang up on me. Thanks to her, I'm here. I'd like you to go and thank her for me."

"I haven't had to contend with so much advice since last time I saw you."

"It's good advice you know." Jake glanced down at his watch and got up. His grin softened into a wistful smile as he took a step closer to Simon. He held out his hand. "I'm sorry, but I've got to go. It was so good to see you again."

Simon took his brother's hand and then, grasping it tightly, pulled him closer. Their arms came around each other and Simon swallowed down a knot of emotion. His brother. His family.

Thank You Lord, he prayed, squeezing his eyes shut.

When he pulled away he could see Jake was as moved as he was.

"I'll walk you to your vehicle."

"That's okay. Let's just say goodbye now. I don't like goodbyes."

Simon held his brother's dark eyes as the unspoken words whispered between them as each remembered other separations, other goodbyes. "I promise this one won't be as long," Simon said, his voice thick with emotion.

Jake smiled back, and then they were hugging again, their arms tight. "Thanks for everything," Jake said pulling back. "You make sure you come."

"I will. I just have some things to do yet. But I'll be there." He hardly dared think past the current moment, that things might work out. He only knew regardless of how Caitlin took it, he had to tell her how he felt.

"Keep me posted," Jake said picking up the overnight bag he'd left by the front door.

"I will." Simon watched as Jake left, closing the door behind him. The visit had come and gone so quickly, but he knew he would see his brother again.

Thank You, Lord, he prayed, closing his eyes in thankfulness. *Now if You could only help me out with this next thing.*

Caitlin leaned against the wall wrapping her arms around herself as she listened to the carolers coming down the hallway of the hospital, fighting down the emotions that were so close to the surface. She blinked, staring ahead at the bright lights that someone had strung along the ward. They swam, sparkled, danced. She blinked again, and her vision cleared.

It was the season, she figured, wiping the tears from her face. Christmas was a time rife with emotions. For Caitlin it was a reminder of how alone she was this Christmas. She smiled at that thought, thinking of all the people swarming through her parents' home, filling it with laughter and noise. Hardly alone.

Her mother had been busy for weeks beforehand, cooking, baking and cleaning in preparation for the holidays. It had been a few Christmases since the three girls were together. Tony and his wife never came.

Where are you, Simon, she wondered closing her eyes, as she dropped her head against the hard wall behind her. Another tear slid down her cheek but she let it go. Are you alone this Christmas? She swallowed a lump that filled her throat. She let herself think of him, pray for him, yearn for him.

Just a few more minutes, she thought, a few more minutes of remembering what he looked like, how his voice could lower and send shivers down her spine, what his mouth felt like on hers.

She bit her lip, clutched her waist harder, knowing she was playing a dangerous game. She was alone and in an hour she had to face her family. She wouldn't have the defenses if she kept this up.

Sucking in another steadying breath she opened her eyes, pushed herself away from the wall and blinked.

Then again.

A tall figure stood five feet away from her, his shoulders hunched beneath a leather jacket, hands in the pockets of blue jeans. Softly waving hair the color of sand touched the collar of his jacket, piercing hazel eyes beneath level brows eyed her intently. His mouth was unsmiling.

Simon.

He's so tall, she thought. She closed her eyes and opened them again. He looks tired. Her thoughts made no sense as she stared, unable to form another coherent thought. Then he started coming nearer and she took a step backward. Immediately she hit the wall behind her, but he kept coming. Finally he was directly in front of her, his deep-set eyes pinning her against the wall.

"Hi, there," he said, his voice quiet. His lips were parted and Caitlin had to clench her fists to keep from reaching up to trace their line, to touch his cheek, to make sure he was real.

"Hi, yourself," she said past dry lips, her heart beating so hard against her chest she thought it would fly out. She had missed him so much, had prayed, had wondered. Now he stood in front of her and she didn't know what to say.

"Caitlin, I need to tell you something," he said with a short laugh.

She looked up at that and saw uncertainty in his eyes, saw two small frown lines between his eyebrows. "Okay."

"I love you," he said, his deep voice surrounding her with its reality, warming her with its sound. "I was wrong. I thought I didn't have anything to give you, but that doesn't matter, does it?"

She shook her head as sorrow and pain and loneliness were washed away by his first three words. "I love you, too," she couldn't help but say.

He closed his eyes, resting his forehead against hers, his fingers lying on her neck. "Oh, Caitlin. I can hardly believe this." His breath came out in a sigh, caressing her mouth, her cheek.

Then his arms were around her, crushing her, pressing her close, his mouth molding and shaping hers. He murmured her name again and again, kissing her cheeks, her eyes, her forehead, her mouth.

Then, he pressed his face against her neck, as he drew out a shuddering sigh.

Caitlin couldn't hold him tight enough, couldn't stop herself from repeating his words back to him. "I love you, Simon. I love you with all my heart." It seemed a weak expression of the fullness in her chest that threatened to turn into tears of happiness.

Simon was the first to draw away, his eyes traveling hungrily over her face. "I can't believe this," he whispered, shaking his head lightly. "I can't believe you said that."

She smiled so hard, she felt as if her face were going to split. She wanted to kiss him again, to throw her arms out and shout it out to the world. I love Simon. Instead she reached up and did what she had longed to do from the first time she had realized her changing feelings for him. She traced the line of his mouth, his beautiful, expressive mouth. Then she pressed her fingers against his lips as if accepting a kiss, then touched her own.

"Okay you two, break it up." A loud voice behind Simon made him whirl around, his arms still holding Caitlin.

Danielle faced them, her head tipped to one side, grinning a crooked grin. "Just because it's Christmas doesn't mean you can flirt with the nurses, Simon."

He looked back at Caitlin, who felt her face redden in response. "I'm not flirting," he said quietly. He dropped a quick kiss on her forehead. "This is serious business." He looked down at Caitlin. "I need to talk to you later," he said his voice full of meaning.

Caitlin looked up at him, her eyes wide at first, then as she understood, spilling over with tears. "Talk to me now," she said softly.

He glanced around the hospital ward. "No. I have a better place in mind."

"Okay, I know what you're talking about," Danielle said with a laugh. "Why don't you head home, Caitlin, and you can put this poor man out of his misery. But first, let me be the first to congratulate you." She gave her friend a quick, hard hug. "Good on you, girl," she said in her ear.

Danielle pulled away and sniffed, wiping her eyes surreptitiously. She gave Simon a quick hug as well, smiling at him as she pulled away. "You take good care of her," she said, a warning note in her voice.

"With God's help, I will," he said, his voice solemn as a vow.

Danielle nodded then turned to Caitlin. "You're not going to be any good to me for the next half hour, Caitlin. You may as well go home."

Caitlin looked up at Simon. "You have to come with me, you know." She waited, almost holding her breath while he seemed to consider.

"I was hoping you'd ask."

Caitlin smiled up at him, her heart full.

Danielle gave her a push. "Just go already."

"Thanks, Danielle," Caitlin said to her friend. "I hope you have a blessed Christmas."

"I will and I know you will, too."

Caitlin nodded, slipped her arm around Simon and together they walked out of the hospital.

The drive back to her parents' place was quiet. Caitlin sat with her head on the headrest of the car, facing him. Simon felt the same way he had that evening sitting by his computer desk. A lightness, a lifting of burdens that had been weighing him down. He drew in a careful breath, trying to find the right words, a place to start.

"I want to thank you for Jake," he said, glancing at her quickly, then back at the road. "He came a few days back. For a visit."

"Thank the Lord," Caitlin breathed, laying a gentle

hand on his arm. She squeezed lightly and it was as if her hand held his heart.

"I thank Him, too." Simon shook his head at the memory. "It was so good to see him again." He bit his lip, knowing that his next words were even more important to her. "I also want you to know that I've done a lot of discovering in the past few weeks. I've discovered a need for redemption in my life, for reconciliation with God." He laughed lightly. "It's been a long road, but I've found the way back. I know I've got a long way to go yet, but for the first time in my life I feel like I'm running toward something, instead of away." He gave her another sidelong glance. "Even though I didn't dare come any sooner than this."

"I'm glad you finally dared." Her fingers touched his cheek, lingering a moment, teasing him, and Simon made a sudden decision. They were on a quiet street and he pulled over.

He put the car into neutral, unbuckled his seat belt and turned to face Caitlin. She sat up straight, her eyes gleaming in the reflected light of the dashboard. Outside, lightly falling snow ticked against the windshield, but inside they were warm, secure. Alone.

He wanted to talk to her but was unable to articulate the feelings that welled up in him. He reached out and almost reverently traced the line of her eyebrows, her cheeks. She turned her face to meet his hand.

"I need to tell you something else."

She opened her eyes, her hand coming up to meet his. "So you said. You're not nervous are you?"

"Yes, I am." He stroked her face, his fingers rough against her soft skin. Did he dare? Was he presuming too much? Maybe, but he also knew for the first time in his life he didn't want to leave, run away. He wanted to stay. Stay with Caitlin.

With shaking hands, he reached into his pocket and pulled out a small velvet box. He took a slow, deep breath and flipped it open.

The solitaire diamond nestled in the box caught the nebulous glow of the streetlights and magnified them, winking out rays of color like a promise.

"I know this is kind of sudden, but I'm scared to wait too much longer. Caitlin Severn, will you marry me?"

Caitlin bit her lip, her eyes suspiciously bright. She looked up from admiring the diamond and let her hands linger down his face, catching him around the neck. "I told you I love you, Simon. I don't know if I can say it enough. I will marry you."

He felt the tension surrounding his lungs loosen at her words. Then he leaned closer, his lips lightly touching hers, their breaths mingling in a sigh. "I want to get to know all about you," he said softly. "I want to laugh with you, to pray with you. Have children. Maybe move into that rambling house we looked at." He slipped the ring on her finger. Then he pulled her close, and then there was no more need for words.

Caitlin was the first to draw away. "We should go. My family is waiting. I want so bad for them to get to know you better."

Simon nodded, nervous again. But he started the engine and drove through the city to her home.

He came to a stop in front of the brightly lit house, festooned with Christmas lights. Caitlin was out of the car and waiting for him as he locked the doors. He came around the front of the car and took her outstretched hand, lifting it to look once more at the ring on her finger. A symbol of commitment. He raised her hand to his mouth, pressing it to his lips.

"Are you sure it'll be okay with your family?" Simon asked as Caitlin tugged on his hand, signalling her desire to go into the house.

"Of course it will be." She opened the door, glancing up at him. "Hurry up. I want my family to share this."

Simon looked past her through the large bay window, its bright light streaming out onto the lawn. Inside, by a colorfully lit tree, Rachel and her husband stood with their arms around each other. Beside them a man he didn't know slept in a recliner, his head tilted to one side, a baby resting in the crook of his arm. A child played at the feet of the embracing couple and as Simon watched, Caitlin's mother walked into the room with a tray of steaming mugs. He could faintly hear Christmas music playing and then the sound of laughter. It looked too good to be true.

"C'mon Simon, what are you staring at?"

He watched yet another moment, wondering again what they would say when he came in with Caitlin as someone who wanted to marry her.

He felt his stomach tighten as it used to all those years ago each time he was introduced to another family, a new place.

But this was Caitlin's family and that made it even more difficult. Now, even more than then, he longed to be accepted, to be a part of that family.

"Did your leg seize up, mister?" Caitlin called out from the porch. "My family is waiting."

Simon gave himself a mental shake, drew in a deep breath and sent up a heartfelt prayer. Then he slowly walked up the steps, through the door and into light and noise and the sounds of an excited family.

"Caitlin, you're here…Caitlin's here…."

"Oh, good… Finally…what took you?" Then a moment's silence descended as the people crowding into the entranceway saw Simon and then the ring on Caitlin's hand.

Then more noise and hugs and cries of congratulation.

He greeted Caitlin's parents as Mr. and Mrs. Just like in all the foster homes, wondering what they would think of him now that Caitlin wore his ring.

"You didn't meet my sister Evelyn and her husband Scott from Portland." Caitlin indicated a couple he hadn't met before. He struggled to commit their names to memory.

Simon drew a deep breath, unconsciously wiping his damp palms down the sides of his blue jeans. He was hugged by Evelyn, shook hands with Scott.

Caitlin caught Simon by the arm as the family moved ahead of them into the living room. "Do you mind if I leave you for a bit? I'd like to change into other clothes."

"You look great just the way you are, Caitlin."

She glanced down at her uniform with a pained look. "Thanks, but I prefer not to look like a nurse at home."

"Go then, but hurry up."

"You'll be okay?"

Simon cupped her face in his hands and brushed a kiss over her lips. "You've got a great family, Caitlin. I think I can manage."

Caitlin pressed her hand to his. "I'll be right back."

Simon watched her run up the stairs, stop at the top, then turn and smile down at him.

He couldn't help but return her smile. Even so, as he entered the living room, he felt a slight touch of panic. This was one family he badly wanted to feel a part of.

"Sit down, Simon. If I know Caitlin, she'll be a while yet." Caitlin's father indicated the couch and Simon sat down, looking around at the family who were trying not to look too hard at him. The first time he'd met them it was only as a friend. Now, he entered their home as a future in-law.

They made small talk. Caitlin's father asked him how his work was going. Simon supposed it was a subtle way of measuring how he would be able to support Caitlin. The talk was stilted for a while and Simon could hardly wait for Caitlin to return.

"Wow, sis. That looks good."

All eyes turned to the doorway as Caitlin walked into the room.

She looks like a ray of light, Simon thought, his heart swelling with pride as she came to his side. She wore a simple red dress made of velvet, short and fitted, accented by a plain gold chain around her neck. Her hair shone, backlit by the light coming from the hallway, framing a face that radiated happiness. He stood up as she approached.

"Sorry I took so long," she said as she came to Simon's side. She brushed her hair back from her face with a casual gesture, the diamond on her finger catching the light from the Christmas tree.

"Long?" Jonathon snorted. "I've seen you take more time to change your mind."

General laughter followed that comment. Caitlin answered in kind and as Simon and Caitlin sat down again, the talk became general.

Caitlin's nephew, Scott and Evelyn's child, came and sat on her lap, her mother passed around the warm cider and noisy talk roiled around the two of them.

Simon felt the tightness in his stomach relax as family business carried on, as if it were the most normal thing in the world for a stranger to come into their Christmas celebration. Scott ended up beside him. Simon found out he had also spent time tree planting and soon they were exchanging hardship stories.

The other family members flowed around them. Evelyn interrupted them to hand Scott the baby. She rested her hand lightly on Simon's shoulder and only smiled at him. Simon felt her acceptance. Rachel gave him a quick hug from behind, Jonathon gave him a curious thumbs-up while Mr. and Mrs. Severn smiled benignly at him and Caitlin.

The Severns were a warm, loving family. The very people he had once derided. He knew he had done it out of self-protection, but now he dared accept what was freely given him.

As he looked around the pleased faces of Caitlin Severn's parents, sisters and brothers-in-law, he knew that with God's help he had discovered a family's love.

He thought of his own brother and his brother's daughter. Another family he was a part of. His heart felt full.

But the best of all was Caitlin tucked into his side, his arm around her, her fingers playing with the solitaire on her hand. He glanced down at her and as their eyes met, he felt as much as saw her slow smile.

She pulled his head closer to hers. "I love you," she whispered in his ear.

Simon felt his heart lift. Would he ever tire of hearing her say that, he wondered? He pressed a kiss to her forehead and drew her even closer.

Someday, he thought, with God's blessing, they would be a family, as well.

Epilogue

"I figured I'd find you here."

Simon's voice from the doorway made Caitlin turn her head. She still wore her nurse's uniform and had meant to change as soon as she got home from work, but she had made a cup of tea and taken it up to their bedroom.

She had paused at the bow window on her way to the cupboard and as she often did, she stopped to look out over the Strait of Georgia, to the hazy blue mountains of the mainland.

"Don't you ever get tired of that view?" Simon teased as he walked up behind her. He slipped his arms around her waist and pressed a kiss to her neck, then nuzzled her ear.

"Nope," Caitlin said, setting her tea cup on the small table beside her. She wrapped her arms over his, leaning back into his embrace. With a shiver of satisfaction she laid her head back against his chest, reveling in his strength, his warmth.

"Why not," he murmured against her hair. "It doesn't change much."

"Of course it does. The morning light makes the water and the mountains look fresh and new. When it rains or storms and the water has whitecaps on it, I feel all safe and cozy in here. In the evening, like now, everything looks so soft and peaceful."

Simon looked up, rocking her lightly. "Every time I see it I think, 'oceanfront property.'"

"Oh, you do not," Caitlin chided, hugging his arms even tighter. "You just say that to get a rise out of me. I know you love this place."

Simon sighed, his chest lifting behind her, his breath teasing her hair. "You see right through me, my dear," he confessed. "I do love this place." He turned Caitlin to face him and she looped her arms around his neck. "But to me the best part of coming to this house is seeing my own dear wife standing at our bedroom window, waiting for her prince to come."

"And he always does." She brushed a kiss over his mouth and laid her head on his shoulder. "But you know the real reason I like to stand at this window and stare out of it?"

"Tell me."

"Because every time I do, you come up behind me, and put your arms around me and my day gets better."

Simon laughed, a gentle rumble beneath her cheek. "You truly are a gift from God, Caitlin Steele."

Would she ever get tired of this, she wondered, holding Simon more tightly. She knew they would have their difficulties. Any relationship came with ups and downs. They'd had their differences already, but worked through them.

But she also knew that their love was founded on God's love. And with His help, their home would be a place of refuge and comfort.

"Let's go have supper," Simon said, drawing away from her.

Caitlin smiled and hooked her arm in his. But as they left, she glanced back over her shoulder, out of the windows to the mountains beyond, praying they might be able to show the same view to their children and, Lord willing, children's children.

Their family.

* * * * *